OK, Joe

OK, Joe

Louis Guilloux

Translated and with an Introduction by Alice Kaplan

THE UNIVERSITY OF CHICAGO PRESS
CHICAGO + LONDON

LOUIS GUILLOUX (1899–1980) was a novelist, essayist, and literary translator of more than two dozen works. He is best known as the author of *Le sang noir* and *Le jeu de patience*, which was awarded the Prix Renaudot in 1949. In 1967, he was awarded the Grand Prix National des Lettres.

ALICE KAPLAN is the author of *French Lessons* and *The Collaborator*, which was a finalist for the National Book Award and the winner of the *Los Angeles Times* Book Prize in history. Her translations include *Another November* and *The Difficulty of Being a Dog* by Roger Grenier.

The University of Chicago Press, Chicago 60637
The University of Chicago Press, Ltd., London
© 2003 by The University of Chicago
Introduction © 2003 by Alice Kaplan
All rights reserved. Published 2003
Printed in the United States of America

12 11 10 09 08 07 06 05 04 03   1 2 3 4 5

ISBN: 0-226-31057-4 (cloth)

Originally published as *O.K., Joe!*, © Éditions Gallimard, 1976.

The University of Chicago Press gratefully acknowledges a subvention from the government of France through the French Ministry of Culture, Centre du Livre, in partial support of the costs of translating this volume.

Library of Congress Cataloging-in-Publication Data

Guilloux, Louis, 1899–
[OK, Joe. English]
OK, Joe / Louis Guilloux ; translated and with an introduction by Alice Kaplan.
p. cm.
ISBN 0-226-31057-4 (alk. paper)
I. Title: OK, Joe.   II. Kaplan, Alice Yaeger.   III. Title.
PQ2613.U495 O513 2003
843'.912—dc21   2002155968

♾ The paper used in this publication meets the minimum requirements of the American National Standard for Information Sciences— Permanence of Paper for Printed Library Materials, ANSI Z39.48-1992.

Translator's Introduction

Louis Guilloux (1899–1980) is among the least known and the most admired French writers of the mid-twentieth century. He was born in Brittany, that northwestern region of France so close in feel to Ireland—the site of Arthurian legend with its pink granite coasts, rich farmland, and magical inland forests. For Guilloux's generation, Brittany was also a place marked by passionate separatist aspirations and limited social mobility. If it hadn't been for his deformed hand—the result of a childhood tuberculosis that affected his bones—Guilloux would have followed his father in a cobbler's trade. Instead, incapable of a hand craft, he was allowed to pursue his studies as a "scholarship boy." Without even having passed the baccalaureate exam, the entryway in France to a university education, he started his working life in a lycée as a monitor, a kind of teaching assistant / dorm resident to the students, and then left for Paris to work as a journalist. As a young writer and intellectual, he made his way in the 1930s on the literary left. He was appreciated by Gide and Malraux, and later by Camus, who wrote: "I love and admire the work of Louis Guilloux, which neither flatters nor disdains the people it portrays and which grants them the only dignity they cannot be denied— that of the truth." In 1967 Guilloux was awarded the Grand

Prix National des Lettres. And in 1999, to celebrate the centenary of his birth, the Théâtre de Folle Pensée in his hometown of Saint-Brieuc staged a marathon oral reading of his 800-page novel, *Le jeu de patience*. Guilloux is still revered today as a writer of deep social commitment, a brilliant autodidact, and, as Saint-Brieuc proclaimed him, "a man of his word."

Louis Guilloux is the author of some two dozen books: novels, plays, and published diaries through which we can trace his activities from 1921, his early Paris years, to 1974, when he began to prepare the manuscript of *OK, Joe*. Some of his books portray life in Brittany, others are concerned with the daily struggle of workers, others with the carnage of war. One novel is set in Italy, a country he loved. All of his work is intensely political.

As a young intellectual in the years of Hitler's rise to power, Guilloux was caught up in the politics of his contemporaries, reeling from the devastation wrought by the First World War and vigilant about the rise of European fascisms. In 1935 he served as secretary to the World Writer's Congress of antifascist writers. He was invited by André Gide on that writer's famous tour of the Soviet Union, a trip that left him disillusioned with state communism and caused his political break with France's leading communist writer, Louis Aragon. The novel that is considered his masterpiece, *Le sang noir*, was published in 1935. Its antihero is a suicidal lycée teacher in the backwaters of Brittany during World War I. *Le sang noir* established Guilloux as a master of despair. An eccentric, a populist, and an internationalist, a regional writer from Brittany and translator of English, American, and Italian literature, a man who shuttled back and forth between his home in Saint-Brieuc and his publisher in Paris but who always lived on the edge of poverty, Guilloux is a contradictory figure, difficult to place in a single literary school or tendency.

We find all of his contradictory appeal in *OK, Joe*, the novella he published only four years before his death. Guilloux constructed his story using the diaries he kept during a brief, intense period from August through October 1944 when he worked as an interpreter for the American army in Brittany. Although *OK, Joe* has both the form and feeling of a fiction, it is remarkably faithful to Guilloux's own experience in its chronology and historical references. Just as he tells it in *OK, Joe*, Guilloux was discovered by army lawyers while working as a translator for the mayor of Saint-Brieuc in the aftermath of the town's liberation. He followed the U.S. army to Morlaix, where hasty courts-martial tried GIs who were charged with crimes. His job was to translate into English the testimony of French witnesses. All but one of the accused GIs he describes in *OK, Joe* were African Americans; most of them were condemned and hanged. The substance of his book lies in that dramatic situation. After serving in several trials, Guilloux left Morlaix with the Americans as they headed across northern France toward Berlin. But in Saint-Quentin, France, he became too ill to continue.

There is much more to his story than even the vivid courtroom dramas at its heart. Perhaps because his book is based on diary entries, Guilloux is able to give us a vital sense of the weeks of August and September 1944, transporting us to the scenes of Liberation. The novel follows the narrator, Louis—based on Guilloux himself—as he wanders through his hometown, rides through the countryside in a U.S. army jeep with a cheerful, efficient driver named Joe, and negotiates his relations with army lawyers and with the witnesses whose traumas he must translate for the American court. *OK, Joe* is a series of vignettes that coheres through Louis's wry perspective, taking its depth from his own subjectivity, beginning with the shock of freedom from the Nazis. Through this personal narration, a lot of history is being told. As the story begins, battles between Americans, free French, and German troops are still under way; collaborators have been arrested by the local Liberation Committee, and women, in particular, are being punished in the streets, their heads shorn by Resistance groups in retribution for sleeping with the enemy: Guilloux watches, listens, and tries to understand. What to make of the Americans? They are, for a man who has endured four years of Nazi occupation, both liberators and new occupiers. The specific American courts-martial he describes are a theater for exposing the contradictions of an army proud of having liberated France from Nazi racism yet quick to make racial assumptions about its own black soldiers. We might infer from his portraiture that as a Breton—always aware of his difference from the mainstream—and as someone specially attuned to the suffering of the poor, he sympathizes with African Americans. He is mystified that they are, with one exception, the only soldiers being arrested. He is also affectionate toward the young Army lawyers he works with, white men who are blind to their own prejudice. Guilloux hears their racism and records it, just as he captures their idealism, which verges on sentimentality.

Beyond its historical setting, what makes *OK, Joe* so appealing to a reader today is its language, beginning with the title. Louis Guilloux is clearly amused and delighted by the peculiar speech patterns of the soldiers he spends his day with. Like many Frenchmen of his generation, he learned British English. The American version of the language was exotic. Guilloux had an extraordinary ear, not just for language but for dialogue and the scenes of speech, and he delights in recording how language tics like "OK" are deployed with near Pavlovian regularity. He explores the sometimes tough, sometimes naïve way the soldiers speak to him and to one another about the war. It is plain speak masking complicated assumptions and biases. In the original French, one of the aspects that contribute to this book's charm is the translation that goes on as part of the story. Guilloux's French text is interspersed with English phrases. His main character, Louis, speaks with the American soldiers, reproduces their idioms in English in italics, then explains to his readers:

> "*Take it easy!*" Autrement dit: "Ne vous en faites pas" ["*Take it easy!*" Which means: "Don't worry about it"].

The French reader comes away from the book with something like a language lesson. This presents a considerable challenge to the English translator, since in English, the "foreignness" of English words no longer stands apart from the rest of the language, and the italics become meaningless. Initially I tried to retain one or two instances where the narrator explains an idiom to his readers, but the result was so awkward that I finally decided to sacrifice Guilloux's pedagogy of translation. Still, what remains for the reader of *OK, Joe* in English is the author's vivid rendition of the idiom of a previous generation of Americans as well as a sense of how odd this sparse American speech sounded to a European ear, accustomed to British diction. For Americans, part of the fascination of Guilloux's prose is hearing our most familiar speech patterns reflected back to us.

Throughout his career, Guilloux was particularly attuned to the process of translation. He studied English only briefly in secondary school, but he liked to practice speaking with the British sailors at the Saint-Brieuc port. During his adolescence, Guilloux was befriended by a British journalist who took up residence briefly in Saint Brieuc; when he was fifteen, he spent two weeks visiting the man's family in England. Still, his mastery of the language is remarkable. He began to work as a translator of English-language dispatches for the newspaper *L'Intransigeant* in the 1920s. One of his first translations was, significantly, Harlem Renaissance author Claude

McKay's *Home to Harlem* in 1932, and he went on to translate over twenty novels from the English, including work by G. K. Chesterton, Cecil Scott Forester, Margaret Kennedy, and John Steinbeck. Translation was piecework for Guilloux, who always lived on a shoestring, but it clearly contributed deeply to his imagination as a writer.

————————

Although the American presence in France has been romanticized in countless books and movies, *OK, Joe* offers us something exceedingly rare: a French perspective on post–D Day GI culture. After landing on the beaches of Normandy on June 6, 1944, the VIII Corps of the Third Army moved westward into Brittany, part of the long march to liberate the whole of Europe from the Nazis. Guilloux recounts several events along the way: the liberation of Saint-Brieuc on August 6, the German counterattacks along the Brittany peninsula, the American campaign to take the port town of Brest from the Germans, and finally the liberation of Brest on September 18. The Allies had bombed the port cities of northern France; they now needed to revive these westward ports in order to bring supplies into France for their march across France and into Germany. Morlaix, in Brittany, became an important American base, a Signal Corps headquarters and a port for supplies.

It may be obvious, but worth emphasizing here, that in wartime and especially in situations of invasion and occupation—even in the act of liberating an allied country such as France—soldiers commit ordinary crimes. Armies bring legal systems with them for handling charges from local communities. This was the case in Morlaix, where the army set up a guardhouse for the soldiers it arrested and operated a General Court Martial—a court of law administered by specially trained personnel within the U.S. Army. In *OK, Joe* Guilloux gives us a vivid picture of the makeshift courtroom, set up in the party room of a local school. GIs charged with desertion, black market activity, assault, rape, and murder were swiftly tried; when their crimes involved French civilians, Guilloux was one of the interpreters brought in to facilitate the hearings.

The story of these GIs is a sad and violent one. In what was known as the European Theater of Operations (including England, France, Luxembourg, Belgium, Germany), 443 death sentences were pronounced by U.S. courts-martial during World War II; 70 executions were carried out. The capital offenses were rape, murder, and rape/murder. Of the 70 men executed, 55 were African Americans. In France, the statistics are even more unbalanced: of 181 soldiers charged with rape, 139 were black. Yet fewer than 10 percent of the American soldiers in Europe were black.

In analyzing these cases, an official army report from 1945 reflects the prejudices of the times, citing low intelligence scores for Negro soldiers and bemoaning the pressure on selective service boards to accept draftees without discernment. The report emphasizes the link between the crimes and hard drinking. In Normandy, for example, soldiers got raw calvados from farmers and did not understand they were drinking 140-proof alcohol—strong enough to work as fuel in their cigarette lighters. The army report is also critical of the regulation forbidding American soldiers from using brothels, citing approvingly the care with which the Germans had designated the cleanest brothel in each town an official recreational center for occupying troops. The report blamed the sex crimes on the received idea of American soldiers that French women, unlike American women, were "loose" and available.

Nowhere in official reports of this kind is there any speculation that rapes committed by white soldiers might have been underreported, although it is clear, when you read the transcripts of actual courts-martial, that many people in Brittany had never seen a person of color and that black soldiers, by their mere presence, engendered fear. How this fear combined with the black soldiers' own behavior is another intangible factor in the outbursts of rage and violence.

In his recent research on GI rapes, J. Robert Lilly, a criminologist, has underlined an important statistic that official army histories report neutrally: most of the men tried for rape were not in the infantry but in the service branches of the army. They worked away from the fighting action, in transportation, food preparation, supplies. The majority of black soldiers in WWII were stationed in service units. Their barracks were segregated; their superior officers were always white. This fact begins to give us a more specific sense of life for these soldiers in newly liberated France—not the excitement of battle but the tedium of service and the misery and humiliation of segregation.

Guilloux served from August 31 through September 29, 1944, as an official interpreter for U.S. military justice. He was hired by an army lawyer named Joseph M. Greene, whom he calls, in *OK, Joe*, Lieutenant Stone. He participated in pre-trial investigations, and, once in the courtroom, he took the interpreter's oath and stood behind the witness's chair, translating testimony directly into English. The trials in which he interprets involve black GIs who were subsequently condemned and hanged for rape or murder. He describes only one case involving a white GI, a Ranger accused of the brutal murder of a French Resistance fighter. This is undoubtedly the most chilling story in his novel. The murder is cold-blooded, the defendant described by an army doctor as "a killer." In this seemingly clear-cut case, Louis is stunned when he is replaced in his role as court interpreter by American intelligence officers. After the Ranger is acquitted, Louis watches him leaving the courtroom with the army lawyers and going to the mess hall to eat lunch with them. Here, as everywhere in *OK, Joe*, Guilloux's own judgment and moral perspective is subtle: we're left to draw our own conclusions about race and the inequality of justice. But we do draw them. Despite the great moral striving and idealism of the American soldiers, theirs is a universe where justice is skewed by racial prejudice. The avengers of Nazism are not without their own flaws.

Wanting to understand more about the trials that formed the basis for Guilloux's story, I began to study transcripts of the courts-martial held in Morlaix, the army base where Guilloux began his work in late August 1944. Reading the actual cases, I immediately recognized the outlines of several stories in *OK, Joe*. In *United States vs. Private James E. Hendricks*, for example, Hendricks follows a young woman home from the base. The court finds that she wouldn't let him in and that he fired at the door, killing her father. In *United States vs. Private First Class William E. Davis and Private First Class J.C. Potts*, Davis and Potts are charged with the attempted rape of a young mother in her home; Davis is charged with murder. Testimony reveals that a neighbor ran to fetch the woman's husband, who was threshing wheat in a nearby field, and that he returned to the scene of the crime. The court finds that in the ensuing struggle, the woman ran away and Private Davis fired at her, killing her.

Guilloux's name appears in the record of the Hendricks court-martial as official interpreter. In transposing the salient details of this court-martial for his fiction, Guilloux changed very little. He does what any good novelist would do: he takes the sources and distills them for his own literary purposes. In the transcript, Hendricks not only fires at the door of one house, he attempts a rape at the neighbor's house next door. When Guilloux fictionalizes the Hendricks case, he leaves out nearly all of the sexually explicit, disturbing detail that comes to the fore in the courtroom. Guilloux's story makes the accused man less repellant, a purer victim. He's tipping the balance so that the reader will be critical of the court. In drawing from another case on the record, what seems to interest Guilloux is not so much the details of the court-martial but a vivid moment in the courtroom, where one French farmer after another is asked to identify the guilty party in a lineup of six black soldiers. In his novella, the scene becomes a slow-motion vision of racial profiling. Guilloux takes the raw material of the trials and transforms it into a drama of cultural misunderstanding, subtler and more heartbreaking than what we can read in the historical record.

Still, these source materials are valuable, not only because they give us a measure of Guilloux's craft and choices as a novelist, but because they give us his voice. When we read in a trial transcript the testimony of a French witness, we are reading Guilloux's simultaneous translation into English. His English is sometimes a little awkward, with a missing article or a slightly fractured idiom. In speaking for the Breton farmers who are victims of American crime, Guilloux's voice is preserved for history. For the translator of Guilloux into English, the record of his own English voice is a precious gift.

Guilloux's novella raises many questions it can't answer. When he works as an interpreter, his contacts are with the army lawyers who investigate the cases and with the families and neighbors of the victims. He has no contact with the accused GIs, no sense of who they are beyond what the army lawyers tell him. The African American men in his narrative are never quoted. They are nameless victims—powerful symbols for Guilloux, and devices for his plotting. He doesn't portray them. *OK, Joe* gives a different picture from any that we have had of the American army in liberated France, and points to many more stories still to be told.

———

In preparing the translation and this introduction I consulted the following works:

Camus, Albert. Preface to Louis Guilloux, *La maison du peuple*, followed by *Compagnons*. Paris: Grasset, 1953.

Denis, Michel, ed. *Louis Guilloux: homme de parole: 1999, centenaire de la naissance de l'écrivain*. Saint-Brieuc: Ville de Saint-Brieuc, 1999.

Guilloux, Louis. *Le jeu de patience: roman*. Paris: Gallimard, 1949.

———. *Salido*, followed by *O.K., Joe!* Paris: Gallimard, 1976.

———. *Le sang noir*. Paris: Gallimard, 1935.

Lilly, J. Robert, and François LeRoy. "L'armée américaine et les viols en France: juin 1944—mai 1945." *Vingtième siècle: Revue d'histoire* 75, July September 2002 : 109–21.

McKay, Claude. *Quartier noir*. Translated by Louis Guilloux. Paris: Rieder, 1932.

I also consulted the following military documents:

United States versus Privates First Class William E. Davis and J.C. Potts. *Board of Review: Branch Office of the Judge Advocate General with the European Theater of Operations*, vol. 11–12, pp. 239–59. Trial convened at Morlaix, France, 23–24 September 1944; reviewed 29 November 1944.

United States versus Private First Class James E. Hendricks. *Board of Review: Branch Office of the Judge Advocate General with the European Theater of Operations*, vol. 11–12, pp. 221–31. Trial convened at Morlaix, France, 6–7 September 1944; reviewed 11 November 1944.

Record of Trial of Private First Class James E. Hendricks by General Court Martial. Tried at Morlaix, Finistère, France, 6–7 September 1944. (Courtesy of J. Robert Lilly.)

Twelfth Army Group (Final After Action Report), vol. 10: *First United States Army, Report of Operations*, Annex no. 15, Provost Marshal Section. Property of Office of the Chief of Military History, General Reference Branch. (Courtesy of Madeline Morris.)

The General Board, United States Forces, European Theater. The
Military Offender in the Theater of Operations. In *Military Jus-
tice Administration in Theater of Operations*, 20 November, 1945.
Study no. 84. Record Group 319, USFET Monographs. National
Archives at College Park, MD.

My thanks go to Yvonne Guilloux, who granted me an interview in
Paris, June 26, 2002. For their generosity and expertise, I am grateful to
Richard Boylan, National Archives; Linda Erickson, Clerk of Courts,
U.S. Army Judiciary; Dan Lavering, Judge Advocate General's School
Library; Robert Gonzales, Judge Advocate, U.S. Army; J. Robert Lilly,
University of Northern Kentucky; and Madeline Morris, Duke Uni-
versity School of Law. I also thank Sara Merkle, Jennifer Rhee, and
Shilyh Warren for their research assistance. Finally, both the introduc-
tion and the text of this translation benefited enormously from the keen
eyes and ears of Cathy N. Davidson, Roger Grenier, Margaret Mahan,
Alan Thomas, and the participants in Laurel Goldman's Tuesday fiction class.

No one in the car was talking, not the two lieutenants in the back, nor the driver I was sitting next to. It must have been around three in the afternoon. We had just left the city hall, where the lieutenants had come looking for me.

As soon as he entered my office, the older one asked me if I was really the mayor's interpreter. When I answered yes, the lieutenants introduced themselves.

"Lieutenant Stone . . ."

"Lieutenant Bradford."

I asked them to sit down. They refused. Lieutenant Stone asked if I was the same person who had spoken with one of their men at the entrance to the girls' school the night before.

He got specific: "With Bill?"

Yes. I was the one. With Bill Cormier, yes.

"OK. According to Bill, it seems you don't have much to do at the city hall?"

That was true too. In fact, I had nothing to do.

"In that case, perhaps you could do us a big favor."

They were about to go out on a case and they needed an interpreter. How about it? The jeep was out in front.

The younger of the two, Lieutenant Bradford, struck me as a large, thirty-year-old teenager, very well groomed, classy, looking rather British—fair hair, a girl's complexion, light blue eyes. He smiled affably. As soon as you saw him, you understood that he must have excellent manners, always and in every situation. His colleague, a little older, seemed sturdier because of his broad shoulders and the way he held himself. Also because of his thick black hair and the stubborn hairs covering his wrists down to the last joints of his fingers. He had beautiful hands, but his facial features were a little coarse, his mouth greedy, his eyes very black. He too was smiling most kindly as he waited for my reply.

I said yes, of course. Why not? But first I had to inform Monsieur Royer, our new mayor, and get his permission. I phoned. Monsieur Royer said I could go, since there was nothing for me to do. And I followed the lieutenants.

The jeep was there, just outside the door, with a driver at the wheel. We got in. The lieutenants sat in back and I sat next to the driver.

"OK, Joe," said Lieutenant Stone.

Joe shifted right into gear and no one said another word.

It wasn't easy to get out of town; there were crowds everywhere, starting with the square in front of the city hall, which is also where the police station is. The crowds had been there from the start, as well as in the center of town, but Joe knew just how to maneuver without losing his patience. As soon as we left downtown, everything went smoothly, and once we got on the road, Joe made good time.

Joe didn't say a word, but he winked at me and passed me a pouch of Prince Albert's. I filled my pipe.

Where were we going? It was a lovely sunny August day. We didn't pass anyone on the road and there weren't any planes in the sky. We drove past the ruins of a burned-out jeep. Joe was a good driver and drove fast. You'd have thought he knew the way as well as one of the locals. He knew where he was going; so did the lieutenants. But I didn't. I hadn't asked, any more than I'd asked what the case was that they needed my services for.

Joe drove for over an hour and then turned left, down a sunken road between steep slopes planted with oak trees. After the bright light of the road there was shade and cool air under the leaves; in the jeep the same silence reigned. Lieutenant Stone was studying a file he had taken out of his briefcase.

We arrived in a hamlet. Joe, still just as sure of himself, drove into a large sunny courtyard. At the back of the courtyard was a small house: four walls and a slate roof. On the wall facing the courtyard was a door, and to the left of the door a window. Joe stopped the jeep. Lieutenant Stone put his file back into his briefcase. He got out first. Lieutenant Bradford followed him. Then I got out. Joe stayed at the wheel.

Lieutenant Stone walked up to the door, briefcase in hand. He knocked. A tall country woman of about fifty, rather stout, dressed in black, opened it. We all cringed at the sight of the woman: her face looked almost as if it had been skinned; her forehead, her left cheek, and her chin were covered with scarlet spots.

"I know who you are," she said softly, stepping aside. "Come in."

The house consisted of a single room with a dirt floor. At the back of the room a young woman was busy tending a stove. She didn't join us.

"Something terrible happened here," Lieutenant Stone told me as he placed his briefcase on the table. "Would you ask this woman . . . ?"

He wanted to find out directly from the witness, "in her own words" as he put it, how she had gotten those lesions on her face.

The woman replied very gently that they came from the splinters of wood the bullet had made when it went through the door.

Lieutenant Stone and Lieutenant Bradford exchanged glances.

"Yes. So that's it," said Lieutenant Bradford.

"And then?" Lieutenant Stone turned back to me: "Ask the witness . . ."

The woman went on to say that the noise of the gun blast had deafened her and that she didn't realize right away that her husband had collapsed at her feet.

"Awful!" muttered Lieutenant Stone. "Just awful."

He sat down at the table, opened his briefcase, and took out a file, which he spread in front of him. Lieutenant Bradford kept walking around the room looking at everything. The girl, a handsome country girl about twenty years old, somewhat heavy-set, with a glowing complexion, stayed next to the stove.

"Ask the witness . . ."

At what time did the incident occur? Had night fallen? Had the girl gone over to the base? Had she spoken to one of the men?

"Ask her . . ."

Yes. The girl had gone to the base.

"Ask her what for."

"To have a look, like everybody else," the mother answered.

They were supposed to be so nice! Why wouldn't she have gone like the others? Everyone had gone.

"Did she speak to one of them?"

"No," said the girl.

"But he followed her," said Lieutenant Bradford as he approached us. "Did he know where she lived?"

"Did he follow you?" Lieutenant Stone asked.

The girl didn't know. She hadn't been aware of it.

After this reply there was another moment of silence. Lieu-tenant Stone threw his pencil down on his papers—he had noted down all of the girl's answers and those of the mother—and leaned back, as if prepared to listen to a long story.

"Now ask the mother to tell us what happened."

The mother looked around; she raised her hand meekly, pointing at the four walls of the room, only one of which had two openings—the door and the window.

"You see. This is where we have always lived. Night was falling. We were getting ready for bed when we heard some-one walking in the courtyard."

At first they thought it was a neighbor coming to ask for a favor or to bring news. But the girl saw the silhouette of a sol-dier through the window. The soldier had called out "Mamoi-selle." The mother had closed the shutters right away while the father locked the door.

"We figured out right away that it was one of the soldiers from the base." The father yelled at the soldier to go away. "There's no Mademoiselle here for you."

Lieutenant Stone wanted to know whether the father had insulted the soldier. For example, had they called him a nigger?

"No, we told him to go away."

Did the witness think that the soldier was drunk at this point?

The mother had no idea. How could she have known? All she could say was that the soldier got mad and started to kick the door.

They were terrified. On the father's orders the girl turned out the lights and hid in a corner next to the wardrobe.

"There," said the mother, pointing to the spot.

More and more enraged, the soldier kept pounding and yelling "Mamoiselle." They thought the door would cave in. The father and the mother leaned against the door and stayed there for a long time, pushing against it.

"How long?"

"I don't know . . . He was pounding hard. First with his feet, then with something else. Father told me to get a hatchet but I didn't dare leave the door."

The mother yelled out to her daughter to get the hatchet. The girl went, but couldn't find it. They had to turn the light back on.

The mother spoke again: "He was pounding with the butt of his gun. Father figured it out before I did."

"For a long time?"

"Yes. Pretty long. The door was shaking. We were still pushing against it. He stopped. We heard him walking and we thought he had left. That's when he fired at the door."

The father had collapsed; half of his skull was blown off. The mother didn't understand right away. She collapsed too, but first she thought that something had fallen on his head, she didn't know, she was dumbstruck. Only later did she realize that she was covered in blood and in her husband's brains and that half her cheek was torn off. From her corner of the room, the girl had started to scream.

"Good. Let's stop there," said Lieutenant Stone. "It's terrible. Absolutely terrible. Tell her we are sorry to have to ask all these questions. Tell her too that the guilty party has been arrested and that he'll be tried in two or three days."

I had the impression no one knew what to say next or what to do. The two women, thinking the officers were finished, offered them a snack. They couldn't refuse a cup of coffee and a slice of bread and butter? They declined politely.

Lieutenant Stone demanded brusquely if they had found the bullet.

"I need that bullet!" he explained, rising from his seat with an air of great authority.

The bullet was clearly somewhere in the room. They had to find it.

"Ask her . . . Ask the witness . . . Ask her if they've looked for it."

"Have you looked for the bullet?"

"Yes, with the neighbors."

"And you didn't find it?"

"No."

"I need that bullet!" Lieutenant Stone said again, with even more passion.

Lieutenant Bradford knelt in front of the door to examine the gash the bullet had made. What was its trajectory? In his opinion, we needed to look behind the wardrobe. Maybe even inside the wardrobe?

But the two women had already searched the wardrobe and hadn't found anything. They had looked everywhere, behind the stove, under the beds . . .

"I must have that bullet!"

––––––––

I let them look for the bullet and went out into the courtyard.

A few neighboring farm people were out there, surrounding Joe, who had climbed out of the jeep and was offering them cigarettes. When he saw me, Joe came over to me, and the people followed him. One of them asked me if they had arrested the guy. I told him they had. They wanted to know who the officers were and what they were doing.

"Investigating. Right now they're looking for the bullet."

Joe knew it was about a murder, but who was the murderer?

"A black man, Joe."

"Dirty bastard!"

"And the officers, who are they, Joe?"

"Military justice. Lieutenant Stone's the prosecutor. Lieutenant Bradford's the defense lawyer."

I explained all that to the villagers. "And who are you?" one of them asked me.

"I'm an interpreter."

"They're not bad guys, the two lieutenants, not bad guys at all," Joe said . . .

A young man came up to me, looking embarrassed. He took an old wallet with a brass clasp out of his pocket and took the bullet out of it.

"Here's the bullet. I wanted to keep it as a souvenir, but I don't want any trouble . . ."

I took the bullet and went back into the house. I gave the bullet to Lieutenant Stone. He cried out, "I've found the bullet!"

Holding the bullet between his thumb and index finger he held it up to look at it and show it off. He put the bullet into his pocket and said, "Excellent!"

———————

On the way back, the two lieutenants weren't at all silent. What a terrible case! Poor people! Poor father! How pitiful! And the murderer barely twenty years old! They'd hang him of course. No one could save him from that. Really terrible! But could you let people get raped and killed? And of course those young black idiots had bird brains. Always ready to go to hell for some white woman! For that they didn't even have to be drunk. And this one probably wasn't drunk that night. He had claimed not to be during his first interrogation. He claimed he never suspected there was anyone behind the door. He hadn't wanted to be mean, he only wanted to teach those people a lesson. When he started following the girl, his intentions were good. That's what he said. Hard to believe all the same. And yet—why not?

He claimed all he had ever wanted was to spend part of the evening with the girl. To have a drink. He would have kissed her if she had let him but that was all. As for the gun he had brought with him, don't forget that American soldiers were forbidden to go out unarmed because of snipers—German holdouts and others who were still roaming around the countryside.

He said he had gotten mad because they were afraid of him. Why were they afraid? Just because he was black? If they had opened the door and offered him a drink, if they hadn't treated him like a nigger . . . It's true they hadn't insulted him, but it was the same thing, and he knew, he knew. Those people would have opened their door to a white man.

Lieutenant Stone kept saying there was some truth to what he said but it was hard to believe it when you really knew blacks. They all said things like that in certain cases.

"Poor guy! But they're all terrible liars, believe me!"

We would come back to get the two women so that they could testify at the court-martial.

"Where did you find the bullet?" Lieutenant Bradford asked me.

"In a neighbor's wallet."

When we were taking leave of one another in front of the city hall, the lieutenants thanked me and invited me to eat with them at the mess if I wanted to meet them at the girls' school at seven. Then we could go to the movies. They'd set up a movie house in the school's party room and they were showing really good films.

As nice as their invitation was, I didn't think I ought to accept. They didn't insist. They told me again how much I had helped them.

"You did a good job!"

They might come back and get me one of these days for another case, if I was willing.

"Goodnight then! See you soon, anyway."

"Sure. See you soon. Goodnight."

"Thanks. See you soon. Maybe tomorrow."

"Goodnight, Joe!"

"OK. Goodnight!" said Joe.

"OK," said Lieutenant Stone, "OK, Joe." And Joe shifted right into gear.

––––––––––

When I got back to the office, I discovered that while I was gone the local commander had come by to see me and that he'd be back the next day around noon. I also learned that a dance was scheduled that evening in the public gardens.

As I was leaving the city hall—it was around six in the evening—I found myself face to face with Bill, a young student from Chicago with whom I'd chatted the day before at the entrance to the girls' school—a huge, friendly guy. Only he was carrying a rifle.

He was coming to see if I wanted to go to the movies. I told him just what I had told the lieutenants.

"Thanks anyway, Bill."

"Really good movies, though," he told me. "So, did you see the lieutenants?"

"Yes I did. They came for me. Why are you carrying a rifle?"

"Orders. Because of snipers. Even if we're only going out for a short time. Well then! The lieutenants—they're good guys, aren't they? Nice guys."

"I went with them."

"Oh? Out on a case?"

"Yes."

"What kind?"

"Murder."

"That's what I thought . . . or something like that. Are you going to stay with them?"

"I don't know, Bill. It's not exactly my line of work."

"Why not? You make a really good interpreter, that's for sure."

"Maybe. I don't know."

"Oh, I see. And what about the victim? One of ours?"

"No. The murderer is. The victim is a farmer."

"Oh! I'm sorry to hear that . . . Terrible. But it's the kind of thing you have to expect, unfortunately. A knife fight? Liquor?"

"No. A girl."

"Oh, I see."

When he learned the murderer was black he said,

"Oh, I see. You shouldn't give guns to those people. They're irresponsible, all of them. Are you going to see the lieutenants again?"

"Maybe."

"OK, hope I see you again! I've got a lot to tell you . . . heaps. I think we'll be here for two or three more days. Are you sure you don't want to come to the movies with me?"

"No, Bill. Thanks though. Not tonight."

"OK, that's fine. Goodnight then. Can you hear the music? What is it? A party?"

"Yes. A dance. In the public gardens."

"Oh, I thought so. See you tomorrow, maybe."

"See you tomorrow, Bill. Goodnight."

"Tomorrow, I hope."

We parted ways at the entrance to the girls' school. Bill ran. He didn't want to miss his film.

In front of the school it wasn't crowded like the night before. It was still too early. But yesterday things had looked like a village fair. A little crowd had gathered and a bunch of Americans were handing out cigarettes, candy, chewing gum, packets of Nescafé to people and joking with the girls. At the door to the school, two soldiers with their arms around each other's necks were singing and tap dancing. From time to time they'd stop and yell, "*We're going to Berlin!*"

"What a change," someone next to me said.

Yes, quite a change from the German guards who had been posted at the same door just yesterday, with their machine guns under their arms, their two grenades in their belts, their dogs.

That was where I first met Bill, right there. A very nice fellow, Bill Cormier. His ancestors came from the Limoges region is what he'd told me first, and if he can he's going to go there to see if he has any cousins left.

He'd asked if I remembered ever seeing the American troops in France during the other war.

"I think they used to call them the 'Sammies,' remember that?"

"In 1917. I remember very well, we called them Uncle Sam's grandchildren."

Bill had seen pictures. The Sammies wore big hats like boy scouts.

"That's right. And today we have helmets. We're not Sammies anymore; we're GIs."

When he heard him talking about helmets, the fellow next to Bill said it was a good thing, since he owed his life to his helmet, and that the day he'd march with the army through the streets of Berlin he was going to paint the German word for "Jew" on his in white letters—"JUDE," this big!—to make them see, those sons of bitches, those dirty bastards . . .

According to Bill, the ones in 1917 were pretty lucky because they didn't get sent to England first.

The Americans hadn't gotten a very good welcome over there, and the English girls were nothing but hussies.

"For sure! They don't even mind going out with blacks!"

Bill seemed like a very good boy, sweet, serious, really decent. A student. What was he studying?

"I'm studying law."

For now he was in the Signal Corps. He didn't know how much longer they'd make their headquarters here, not more than a couple of days, but he really hoped to see me again. There was so much to talk about.

"Why not, Bill? Come by the city hall. Ask for the mayor's interpreter. I don't have much to do, you know."

"OK. As soon as I can, I'd really like to. Listen, I'll tell you about our bishop."

Just before the troops left for Europe there was a religious ceremony, and the bishop, admonishing the young soldiers, said to them: "My boys! If you're going over there to keep the world the way it is, then you might as well stay home! But if you're going to change the world, then go!"

Bill thought the bishop was damn right. They were going to change the world, that was for sure. Hitler was screwed. In two weeks Patton would be in Berlin.

———

. . . I let Bill run off to his movie, and I wandered down to a rotary at the end of the street and sat on a bench. Here, one step removed from the center of town, no one was around. That was what I wanted. And I still had some time left before I had to go back to the inn where I had been staying for nearly two months. My family was away in the country. This inn is an old-fashioned place; you can get food and drink, you can arrive on foot or by horseback, as the ancient signs on the wall still say, and there's a giant cork hanging over the door. The owner is a woman from the country who wears the traditional Breton headdress. It's called the Auberge de l'Espérance—the Inn of Hope. Nearly all the guests are construction workers: masons, plasterers, carpenters. I've always felt at home there.

———

It seemed as though I were sitting on that bench for the very first time, looking out onto the vast landscape of valley and fields with the sea in the distance, though it's a landscape I've known since childhood and have always loved. It felt different somehow, and yet I could see that nothing about it had visibly changed. There was still the same village clock, the same remains of an old feudal tower on a knoll, the same charming valley with a narrow creek flowing through it; I could hear the murmur of the water in the silence of the evening. How could I be watching it all with this feeling of indifference, how could I be sitting there so calmly on that bench—something I hadn't done for years? I was almost without thoughts, almost without memories, like a foreigner. I might have stood up, taken a few steps along the path that looked out over the valley, leaned over the railing to see the poplar trees along the stream below. But did I really want to? What was going on? Until now, despite the fatigue and the hardships of the past four years, I'd never experienced anything like this. Where did this uncanny sensation come from, like the fantastic vision I had one night just after the Liberation, when I passed by a wide open window and saw, in the bright light, an entire family having dinner around a table. That seemed incredible to me, and I told myself we would have to relearn many more things than we ever thought. And doing that would take time.

The war wasn't over. D Day had been a success, but many Germans were still resisting, in Saint-Malo, in Brest, in Lorient. And Paris wasn't liberated yet. We'd have to wait a while longer before we could allow ourselves any new hope. And in the meantime, was I going to spend my days in that office in the city hall with nothing to do? Maybe the American lieutenants would come back and ask me to go out with them on some new case. It wasn't really my kind of thing. The memory of what I had seen and learned in the hamlet horrified me. Despite the pity I felt for the victims, and for the guilty party too, the one they were going to hang, I'd felt out of place. As for my own work——my writing——I'd lost interest in it ages ago.

Among the vague thoughts that passed through my head that night, what Bill had said about his bishop kept coming back to me: "My boys, if you're going over there to keep the world the way it is, then stay home, but if you're going to change the world, then go!" Yes, that bishop was right, but you didn't have to be a bishop . . .

. . . Vague thoughts, indeed. I felt I was going to have to re-learn how to relax, to break out of the curious apathy I was in. Where was I? Where were we? Everything had happened so quickly. How many days had passed since the American troops arrived in town? How many since the Germans had left?

One morning at the beginning of August, very early in the morning, I was awakened by violent explosions and saw thick smoke rising above the town. The Germans were starting to destroy their ammunition depots. One of those depots was in the lycée, which blew up and caught on fire. As I thought about it, this seemed to have happened a long time ago; it seemed a very long time since that morning I had spent in town in the middle of the crowd running through the streets, shouting all manner of things, the crowd that had already started pillaging the offices of the collaborators and had stormed the warehouses and whose anger doubled when someone discovered that the Germans had soaked what was left of the flour supplies in gasoline. At the top of our main street, the rue Saint-Guillaume, the bookstore for German propaganda had been ransacked. The shop windows had been smashed with paving stones and everything in it destroyed, torn up, thrown into the streets—the books with their incendiary titles, the piles of *Mein Kampf*, the posters with swastikas, the giant portraits of Hitler and of Göring—everything was trampled on, thrown out, or taken away. The street was strewn with pieces of glass and torn books. Next door, beneath a balcony, hung portraits of Hitler and Laval as if they were on a gallows.

Standing in front of a printing press where people were waiting in line to buy colored paper for making flags, we suddenly heard the sound of a machine gun coming from the public gardens. Germans? Snipers? Who was it?

All afternoon we heard explosions and machine guns firing. A battle had taken place on the road to Paris between Resistance fighters and the Vlassovs—Russians who had collaborated with the Nazis. At the port there were still four German speedboats patrolling from Saint-Malo. A number of explosions could be heard from the port. People said that there were still over five hundred Germans in the area and also that the locks were supposed to blow up as soon as the patrol boats went out to sea at high tide.

Overlooking the port and the bay from the Aubé knoll at nine in the evening, I saw the German installations on the coast in flames. Flaming with brilliant colors at sundown. Since the tide was high, I saw one of the four patrol boats going out into the channel.

These images came back into my mind in the most confusing way, in no particular order, sometimes even without any connection from one to the other, like dream fragments, and I couldn't have said on what day, or where, or on what street or square I had witnessed this or that event, or why I had been struck by certain details apparently without any great importance but which I had known right away I would never forget. All I knew for sure was that the Germans hadn't left the same day they started their destruction and that on that day the

American troops were still far from making their entry into the city. It took them another three days after the Germans left, three days during which the Russian collaborators were still shooting at the borders of the city, holding out against the Resistance.

All that had already happened. The scenes of anger and pillaging had given way to a jolly party atmosphere, to a profusion of flags on windows and monuments, to singing and dancing in the streets. The crowd was there, now applauding loudly as a truck passed by filled with bare-armed young men carrying rifles and machine guns, now screaming with hatred at the sight of two policemen taking a man in handcuffs off to prison. Arrests were being made, houses were searched, women suspected of sleeping with German soldiers were having their heads shaved. Here and there, especially in the former headquarters of the German High Command, transformed into permanent offices for the Front national,* grisly documents were displayed: photos of the mass graves that had just been discovered, images of young men and women taken into the woods, massacred with shovels and axes and set on fire, or torn to pieces as if by wild animals; images of prison camps; other images of women drinking champagne with German soldiers. Crowds formed, crying out for vengeance. On the Champ de Mars huge piles of paper burned slowly, the smoke rose into the sky: the archives of the German High Command that the Germans themselves had set on fire before they left.

So that was history, the great moments of history, already memories! Images. A photo of Hitler, pinned to a tree trunk, dirty, full of holes, with a Resistance cross of Lorraine drawn on it in lipstick, and at the bottom, also in red, the inscription "The Germans are the victors on all fronts." People passed

*A confederation of Resistance movements dominated by the Communist Party; not to be confused with Le Pen's postwar National Front party.

by, smiled, shrugged, spit on the photo. Others burst out laughing.

The photo falls down, the wind carries it off; no—it's displayed on the sidewalk. A man stops, thinks for a moment, and then, with his nose in the air, wipes his feet on the photo. Another image: a French sailor wearing a German sailor's boots and holding a German sailor's cap, its ribbons floating . . .

∀

At the Espérance, I'm sitting next to old Charbonnier; he's dying for me to read the latest letter from his son, who's been working in Germany since 1942. I decline. He insists. Finally I take the letter and pretend to read it. Then I give it back to him.

"Well, do you see? He's my best boy!"

He wants to show everyone the letter.

"What's that? A letter from someone special?"

"No: a letter from my son who's been working in Germany since 1942. It was right before Christmas when he left, I was miserable."

At the back of the inn a hulking guy, sixtyish, very drunk, stands in front of the bar and throws the change the waitress has given him on the floor.

"Pick it up," he says, his voice slurred. "It's for you. I don't care about the money. Pick it up!"

That makes everybody laugh.

"Monsieur Morin," says the waitress as she picks up the change, "your daughter is waiting for you."

The old man tightens his cap. He waves his hand in front of his nose as though he were shooing away a fly.

"Pick up the rest!"

She picks up the change. But Morin wants another drink. One last drink. She doesn't want to serve him. They argue. No one pays them any mind. Nor does anyone care about old Charbonnier's letter, which he quietly folds up and puts back in his wallet.

Old Charbonnier leans toward me.

"Isn't it true," he whispers in my ear, "that education is worthless today? I can tell even from the homework they're giving the kids . . . it's worthless . . ."

A young man walks past the inn, whistling the *Internationale*. Someone gets up from the table and asks if there are any potatoes left—a young man who came to work in France back when Mussolini marched on Rome. He's strong and handsome, a quiet Hercules. He comes from a place near Venice. He's a day laborer.

"No more potatoes?"

"No, Angelo," the waitress replies, smiling.

"Oh well!" he says, returning the waitress's smile with one of his own.

And he leaves.

American tanks paraded through town all day. They were headed toward Brest.

We heard a noise, and since the door of the inn was wide open, we saw a car stop right in front. A whole group of young men, some wearing their Resistance armbands, leaped out of the car. There were at least six or seven of them. I thought they were coming in, but they didn't. Two of them disappeared into the hallway next to the inn; we heard them running upstairs. The others waited below.

Everyone came out of the inn. We heard little screams, and the men came hurrying back down. They reappeared, pushing a girl in front of them. One of the men who was waiting went into the inn, picked up a chair, and set it down on the sidewalk against the wall. The men made the girl sit down; she was around twenty, a short, skinny little maid from the inn. One of the young men held her head down and started to chop off big clumps of her hair with a large pair of scissors.

Another stood nearby, holding a razor.

One of the young girl's legs was shaking as violently as if she were pedaling a bicycle. Around her, people were laughing and joking.

"Don't worry. Two months from now, she'll be working in the whorehouse."

"Don't shake like that!"

"You didn't shake like that when you were sleeping with the Boches."

"Cut her hair short."

"Hey man! He's doing it like a real hairdresser."

"Look, I know how to use a gun, not scissors."

She lets them do it, tilts her head to the right, to the left, gently obeys the hand that's pushing her. Brown locks collect around the chair. Her knee is still shaking.

She murmurs something so softly that the guy with the scissors stops working and leans down toward her ear.

"What? What are you complaining about? You can tell the captain we don't give a fuck. Tell him we shit on him."

Everyone else cracks up.

"Should we take her on a little tour?"

When she heard that, the girl leaped up from her chair.

"Easy, now!" yelled the man with the scissors, and put his hand on her shoulder.

"Should we take her?"

"I don't know . . . we'll see. Stop moving, for God's sake."

"All right! All right! That's enough! Don't hurt her."

"I'm not here to hurt her, I'm here to humiliate her. Didn't that occur to you? Wait! It's not over. A little shave now. Pass me the razor."

He takes the razor from his helper, who is still standing

next to him, and gives him the scissors. In what's left of her hair he shaves a cross of Lorraine. Then he stands back and says: "Look! You're a beauty! Get up! Climb onto the chair!"

When she neither answers nor moves, he repeats his order twice. Swearing.

"God damn it!"

She manages to climb onto the chair just as he is threatening to help her. She stands up very straight, with a strange smile, focusing on no one. Her shaven head grotesque and terrible.

"Yell 'Vive la France!' "

She tries. Her lips barely move.

"Louder!"

"Vive la France!"

"Yell 'Down with the Boches!' "

She yells as loud she can.

"Down with the Boches!"

"Now applaud!"

She doesn't seem to have understood; the circle of men moves in.

"Applaud for God's sake or we'll make you . . ."

She strikes her hands together twice without making any noise.

"That's good. Now get the hell out of here. And no wig!"

She jumps off the chair and dives into the hallway. The guys jump back into their car and disappear.

Nothing but the chair by the wall, and on the ground, around the legs of the chair, the brown locks like birds' feathers, beginning to blow away in the evening breeze.

Returning to the office, I found a set of multicolored objects on the table, and Michel, the young man I share this office with, told me, "They're for you."

There were all sorts of brightly colored boxes, some cardboard, some metal: rice, cocoa, tobacco, cigarettes, chewing gum, Nescafé, candy . . .

"An American brought you that stuff . . ."

From Michel's description, I knew it was Joe.

"He left you a note, too."

Joe's note informed me that he was returning today to the same hamlet to pick up the mother and daughter so that they could serve as witnesses in the murder trial. Then Michel started to tell me how he went to the celebration the night before. It was great. A lot of people were there: at least twenty musicians on the stand, which was decked out with a lot of flags. They played various national anthems, starting with the American, then *God Save the King*. Michel was very surprised: he had expected the *Internationale*, in honor of the Red Army. Instead of the *Internationale*, the orchestra had played the *Song of the Volga Boatmen*. After the *Song of the Volga Boatmen*, a beautiful girl mounted the stand—she was holding the French flag, which she draped around herself—and sang the *Marseillaise*. The whole crowd joined in the refrain; the men took off their hats; the soldiers stood at attention. Michel noticed two officers from the Royal Air Force in the crowd. It was a moment he would remember for the rest of his life.

When he'd finished describing the evening, Michel told me he was going to be married soon. Couldn't we think about getting married, now that it was over?

Why not?

How does Michel keep busy at the office? He's never told me and I've never asked. People come to see him, he has them fill out papers and sends them to another office.

. . . An American officer came in, and I could see right away that he wasn't in a good mood. He was the "town major," the local commander, a short man, no longer young, dry, grouchy. They'd told him he'd find an interpreter here. He wanted to visit the airstrip.

"Are you the interpreter?"

"Yes."

"OK."

We went in a jeep. When we got to the airstrip, the guys started waving us down.

"Stop!"

We stopped. The guys told us to be careful and to drive only on the runways.

"Before they left, the Krauts set up mines everywhere except for the runways. Tell that to your Yankee."

I told the local commander. He replied he didn't give a damn. We drove everywhere, any old way. We didn't get blown up. And then we left. At that point, the local commander asked me if I could help him find a horse.

"I want a horse!"

I drove him to the barracks. Commander Pierre would be there.

The barracks were full of FTP and German prisoners.*
The prisoners were sweeping the courtyard. I asked for Commander Pierre, and he emerged looking like a man who was being disturbed. I introduced him. The two commanders saluted one another.

"He wants a horse."

"What are you telling me? A horse?"

Where did we think he was supposed to find a horse?
The local commander wants a horse. He has to have a horse. He's used to riding every day. But there aren't any horses here. Isn't he from the United States? Well then . . .

In the end, Commander Pierre promised to find him a horse and bring it to him the next morning.

"OK."

The local commander drove me back to the city hall. As we were parting, he asked me why we had so many political parties in France. In America there were only two . . .

Someone was waiting for me at the office: my friend Bertrand's sister. A woman of about thirty, quite frail, very sweet, defenseless, gracious, fine-featured, quite thin, with chestnut hair and blue eyes. Not wealthy, though she had been once.

She had come to tell me that they had arrested her brother that morning. Two men had showed up at their door early. They were looking for Bertrand to take him to the camp at Langueux. Bertrand let himself be taken without protesting. They didn't rush him. The policemen suggested he bring a blanket.

She finished with tears in her eyes and said: "But they promised us . . ."

Yes, of course! I could testify to that since the promise had been made to me and I was the one who was supposed to transmit it to him. That was only three days ago. And who had made

*FTP stands for Francs-Tireurs Partisans (a communist resistance movement).

me the promise? The president of the Liberation Committee himself, Monsieur Avril, known as Tonton—the underground name a few of us still called him by.

"Tell Bertrand not to worry . . ."

I could still hear Tonton telling me that as I left, and adding that I could inform Bertrand. What had happened? Tonton was a man of his word.

I promised Bertrand's sister that I would return to police headquarters that very morning; I hoped to see Tonton right away.

"Go home. I'll let you know what Tonton says—but in the meantime you must realize that this has got to be a misunderstanding."

Tonton's waiting room at police headquarters was full of silent people who had come to plead their own case or that of some imprisoned relative or friend—all kinds of suspects. An emaciated old lady from a good family, dolled up in mourning clothes with big black eyes behind her dotted veil, was standing in a corner near a window—a wealthy bourgeoise, usually rather haughty, who I knew had come because her son had been arrested the day before. Why did she insist on standing? She was the only one; all the others were sitting.

I knew them all a little, and I knew what each of them was doing there. A certain Monsieur Delorme, for example, a journalist and lecturer, an occasional actor, aged forty-five or fifty, with an intellectual demeanor, very elegant but a bit foppish, was there for his own sake but especially for his son's.

When I entered, everyone looked up at me then immediately turned away. Some made a slight gesture as if to say hello. It's not always easy to feel on the right side. The bailiff didn't ask me to fill out the forms. He winked at me and went into Tonton's office. A second later he came back and opened the door for me. I walked through the waiting room without looking at anyone. Tonton was at his desk. Christian,

François, and Lavoquer were there. The three of them were gathered around a table, hunched over some papers; Lavoquer was seated, Christian and François were standing.

"What brings you here?"

"Bertrand. He was arrested this morning."

"Which Bertrand?" Lavoquer cried. "That little asshole? Always in cahoots with the Boches."

"Wait!" said François. "Let's see if he's on the list."

They were, at the time, just looking at a list of suspects. Tonton thought they were arresting too many people. They needed to release as many as possible.

"Of course he's on the list!" said Lavoquer.

"So cross him off!" Tonton replied. "And you," he went on, talking to me, "how did you find out?"

"His sister came to see me."

"You tell his sister that I'm going to take care of this myself. I'll see if they dare treat me like this. I called the commissioner right away after I saw you. He promised me faithfully . . ."

"Good, I'm crossing him off," said Lavoquer. " . . . Still, people who wanted a German victory . . ."

"He did plenty for us," Tonton said. "Just ask Pierre. Cross him off."

He crossed out Bertrand's name. Nothing left for me to do but leave.

"Wait," says Christian. "You must come over to the labor office with me. I want to look over Routier's papers with you. There are photos too. We have to look at all of it, his records too. Oh yes, as far as Bertrand is concerned, go see Gaubert."

Gaubert is a police inspector and a solid member of the Resistance.

The bailiff brings in Monsieur Delorme, the journalist and lecturer. Right away, Monsieur Delorme starts bragging.

"But sir, I gave anti-German talks before the war."

To which Christian replies that that's quite possible but

has nothing to do with his attitude since then, nor with the fact that his son went to Russia to fight for Hitler in the Legion of French Volunteers.

"Come over to the Front national with me, then. You'll have to do a better job of explaining yourself."

––––––––––

. . . As I was leaving I saw the old lady in mourning garb, still standing, stiff as a china doll in an antique-shop window. She certainly could have sat on the chair that Monsieur Delorme had just vacated. Maybe she didn't want to.

Then I went to see Inspector Gaubert.

"You know they arrested Bertrand this morning?"

He didn't know.

"Despite what Tonton promised."

He shrugged.

"It's very simple," he replied. "No one realized the arrest warrant was still circulating. It was a piece of paper that had to be voided . . . Don't worry. I'll take care of it. Bertrand will be back home in no time."

At which point he started saying he couldn't take it anymore. Day and night, out on cases.

"It's too much! Again this morning, I went to interrogate a woman. A strange story—but that's not the point—I spent an hour questioning her. The bitch! I couldn't make her cry! . . ."

Think what you like, but a cop will always be a cop . . .

––––––––––

When I went back to the Espérance, I saw that the chair wasn't on the sidewalk anymore and that the last lock of hair had been swept away. No one said much at dinner about the girl they'd shorn last night, except that she hadn't been seen since.

––––––––––

They say that Saint-Malo has fallen but the city is in flames. In Brest and in the Lorient area, heavy German contingents are holding out. Quimper and Vannes were apparently liberated by French troops. The Americans are supposed to be in Nantes, in Angers, in Chartres, even beyond. They're said to be less than seventy-five kilometers from Paris. Meanwhile you can hear the cannon fire not far from here, around Cape Fréhel, where, they say, there are still some small German units defending themselves. In town it's always the same buzz, the same parades of tanks, cars, trucks. A truck full of FTP marches to the cheers of the crowd, greeting them with two raised fingers: V for Victory!

In a nearly deserted street I saw a man, not rich but the kind who lives off his investments, who had stopped in front of a closed-up shop. On the sign in front of the shop was the owner's name in big letters: "Arthur Weber, Antique Dealer," and on the wooden shutters, written in chalk, the word "Fled."

The man is planted there, cane in hand, a small-time investor just as in the old days. Sixty or sixty-five years old, yellow shoes with beige spats, striped pants, black jacket and vest, a watch chain hanging from one pocket to the other, a starched collar and a blue tie. Spick and span. A gray felt hat. Cuffs. And a ruddy, slightly flat face, a full mustache and a goatee.

"Personally," he said when he saw me, "I don't like a name like that"—he pointed at the sign with his cane. "He's one of those who took advantage."

A woman stopped to look. She wasn't wearing a hat.

"But you don't know," she says. "What does a name prove, anyway?"

The investor turns toward her, furious, and the woman walks away.

"Did you hear her? Well now! I respect her sex. I don't have the privilege of knowing you, Monsieur, but I live off my investments. I was in the wine business. A traveling salesman. So you understand. My wife would say to me, 'Come on now! Sell some of this, sell some of that . . .' And all that time those people . . . and we're supposed to feel sorry for them? For God's sake!"

He strode off, holding his cane up high.

Just as he promised, Christian came to my office in the city hall around four in the afternoon to go over to the labor office together as we'd planned. First he told me, which he hadn't had time to do that morning, that Routier, whose papers we were going to see, had been under arrest for four days and that he would receive a proper trial.

We got into a very nice official car, Tonton's car, driven by his chauffeur—a car and chauffeur which, barely eight days before, had been the Vichy prefect's car and chauffeur.

. . . We went into Routier's former office; Christian took a ledger out of a cupboard, put it on the table, and said, "What do you make of this?"

What I saw was a kind of medieval-looking manuscript illustrated with ink sketches that resembled children's drawings of castles, knights in armor, soldiers. I leafed through it . . . it was the same all the way through. The script, which looked indecipherable, was in gothic lettering. The lists of names were also in gothic script. Here and there, clippings from the German press or portraits of Nazi generals had been pasted in.

"So you see. He really was nuts."

"Yes, I see."

"And it's a nut case like that who turned in ten Frenchmen a day to Hitler for his obligatory work service!"

He put the ledger back in the closet, and we left.

————

Around six in the evening, Lieutenants Stone and Bradford came back. It was Lieutenant Stone who explained the purpose of their visit. If I wanted, I could go off with them as their official translator. I'd have an official appointment with army headquarters. But I needed to decide right away. Headquarters was leaving town. Joe could pick me up and take me to Morlaix, where headquarters would stay until the Brest campaign was over.

"Now it's up to you!" they said.

I told them I needed to see the mayor first.

"OK," said Lieutenant Stone. "Joe will come for you to-morrow."

After the lieutenants left, I went to talk to the mayor in his office. I saw that the statue representing the Republic, which the Germans had taken down when they arrived, June 18, 1940—that would be four years and two months ago—had been put back on its stand. It was the mayor who pointed out the bust. So who had sent me? I told him. He answered that he understood completely, adding that I could certainly be of more use to the Americans than I would be if I stayed here in the office, yawning.

What did I do next? I took a walk. I went to sit for a moment on the bench down at the rotary, waiting until it was time to go back to the Espérance.

I told myself it would probably be better to refuse to leave with the Americans. I didn't want to go. I didn't feel capable of doing what they were asking. I should have gone home and gotten back to my own writing, though I doubted I'd ever be able to. I might get back to it someday, but I'd need time. I felt like a stranger to myself and to everything, overcome with a sense of total uselessness.

A little later, after my meal, as I was leaving the Espérance, I was witness to a violent scene.

———————

A crowd has formed on the boulevard. Two men have just shown up in front of a modest house with a garden in the front yard and an iron gate. The younger of the two men—a twenty-year-old—is standing in front of the gate and blocking the opening with his arms spread wide. He's in shirtsleeves with his sleeves rolled up to his elbows; he's wearing an old World War I helmet. He's laughing. The other man—around forty—climbs the few steps that lead to the stoop in front of the little house. He pounds on the door with his fists. No one answers. On the boulevard the crowd is growing. The man, enraged, leans to the right to pound on the windowpane. Below him the other man keeps laughing.

Suddenly the door opens, and a man around fifty appears, tall and thin with white hair and a cap, wearing blue coveralls. Someone in the crowd murmurs, "The father!"

"Are you deaf?" yells the angry man.

To which the man in blue coveralls replies calmly that he isn't. And the angry man asks, "Where is she?"

There's no response. Without turning around, the father shuts the door behind him and plants himself in front of the other man.

"What do you want from her?"

The man grows even angrier. He yells, "You know what I want? She's a whore. She collaborated. I'm coming to arrest her. Where is she?"

"Wait a minute! Wait a minute now!"

"A minute, huh? Hold on!"

He puts his hand in his pocket. He's about to take out a pistol.

"You're crazy," the father says. "Quite crazy!"

"I'm counting to three!"

"Are you nuts?"

"One!"

"Are you kidding?"

"Two!"

The father turns toward the people who are watching. "You'd let him do this?"

No one budges.

The father turns away from him and stands straight against the door, waiting, while the other man, who has taken out his pistol, counts to three.

"Let me in. You've no choice. I'll say it again, when I get to three . . ."

But suddenly there's drama. The door bursts open, and a tall, beautiful brunette appears, around twenty-five, well built.

"Go ahead, then," she says. "Count to three. What are you waiting for?"

An old woman pokes her head through the open door—the mother. She grabs her daughter by the skirt.

"Come back here! Are you crazy? Get back inside!"

The man with the pistol and the father look at each other, equally taken aback.

"Fine!" the father says. "No reason for me to go to any trouble."

"What is it then?" says the young woman. "You want to kill me?"

The man with the pistol doesn't know how to respond.

The mother is still pulling at her daughter's skirt. The daughter turns to her: "Get your hands off me!"

The mother lets go of her and retreats. The father looks at all the people again and says, "You'd better go on home!"

"That's what you think!" the young woman exclaims. "They love this."

"Tell me," she says to the angry man, "do you have orders?"

The poor idiot replies that he doesn't. The father slaps his thigh. "That's the last straw! No orders!"

But the other man shouts that he'll have his orders tomorrow, and that until then no one should leave the house. "You understand?"

The fellow comes down off the stoop, his pistol still in his hand. Before he reaches the bottom step he turns around and says to the girl: "Because you're nothing but a whore!"

"Not with you, as you well know!" she answers, pulling her father back into the house.

She slams the door behind them. The young man in the helmet, his arms still spread wide across the garden gate, is still laughing. Before leaving with his buddy, he calls out to the crowd: "Buzz off!"

They went back that night but they went to the wrong door. They banged and knocked at the neighbors', two spinsters who were scared to death. When they got no answer, they broke down the door, and when they realized their mistake, they went next door. But the one they were looking for had fled with her parents through the back yard. They asked for help from a neighbor, who refused. Father, mother, and daughter spent the night in a shelter, and finally they turned themselves in to the authorities.

Yesterday we learned that after four days of fighting, Paris has been liberated. In addition, they're announcing that Vichy has been captured by the Forces françaises de l'Intérieur.* The allied armies who landed in the south continue to advance. The Americans are at Lens . . .

. . . This morning when I got to the city hall I found Joe waiting for me. He was trying to explain something to Michel,

*The Forces françaises de l'Intérieur (or FFI) were armed Resistance fighters within France—as opposed to the Free French in London.

but since neither had made himself understood, they were both laughing.

What Joe wanted to know was why there were so many political parties in France. In the United States there were only two. That was the same question the town major had asked me. I translated the question for Michel. He burst out laughing and threw up his hands. Why so many parties? He had no idea. He had never wondered why. That was how it was. And I told Joe his question was rather difficult to answer.

"Well then! Lieutenant Stone sent me."

"I know. He came to see me yesterday evening with Lieutenant Bradford."

"Yes, I know. And now you know that the court-martial is set for tomorrow or the day after. So I'm here to pick you up. Apparently you have to see the mayor?"

"I've seen him."

I was just as undecided as the day before. Nonetheless, I answered, "OK, Joe."

The jeep was in front of the door.

"OK, Joe."

He shifted into gear.

———

The trip took us about an hour. Joe didn't say much. It was a beautiful day. Once we got into town, Joe went right toward the school where the headquarters was already set up. The courtyard in front was already full of soldiers coming and going, and in the other courtyard, behind the buildings, were the garages and the vehicles for the Signal Corps.

Bill must be nearby.

Joe stopped the jeep in the rear courtyard. When I turned around after getting out, I saw that there was yet another courtyard—the continuation of this one, and that the two were separated by barbed wire, with military policemen armed with rifles standing guard along it.

Just then some planes flew by, very low. A moment later we heard bombs going off. Joe looked up at the sky, shrugged, and lit a cigarette.

"Brest!" he said as he peered over his match before blowing it out and tossing it.

"What's here, Joe? The prison?"

"Sure, it's the prison. You can tell from the barbed wire and MPs."

Behind the barbed wire a few prisoners were playing ball. They were all wearing shoes without laces. None of them was wearing a jacket. Almost all were colored. "Say, Joe, is this a special prison for colored men?"

"No. It's the prison."

"And they're playing ball?"

"Why not? You know, this is where the guy who murdered the girl's father is. He'll plead guilty."

"And then?"

"He'll be hanged."

No one could save him. Joe took a long drag on his cigarette and walked off saying, "It's a prison, all right!"

He turned around and pointed at the two lieutenants, who were coming to meet me.

"Hello!"

"Hello!"

"By the way," Lieutenant Stone said as he shook my hand, "my name is Robert. Call me Bob—everyone does."

"And my name is William," said Lieutenant Bradford as he held out his hand in turn. "Call me Will."

"And what's your name?"

"Louis."

"OK, Louis."

All very cordial, light-hearted, good-natured.

"And this is where you have your prison for colored men?"

My question startled Lieutenant Stone—I mean Bob.

"Oh, Louis! What are you thinking!"

This prison was for everyone. If there were mostly blacks there, it was because they deserved it.

"And you allow them to play ball?"

"Why not?"

"I'm going to walk around," said Will. "We'll meet up at the mess."

"OK, see you soon, Will. Let's walk around too," said Bob. "Maybe we'll run into Bill, he couldn't have gone far."

The vehicles for the Signal Corps were in a corner of the courtyard. We could hear their motors humming.

Bob had taken care of the two unfortunate women that Joe had brought in from the hamlet. He had checked them into a hotel that was supposed to be one of the best in town. I would see them the next day at the court-martial.

"At nine tomorrow morning. The trial starts at nine. Come on, Louis, I'll show you the room you'll sleep in tonight."

How does he manage to move around everywhere with such ease, in places he's never been? Like Joe on the tiniest country road. Without the slightest hesitation he had me take a right, then a left, go up one staircase, down another. When he opened a door, it was always the right one. He didn't have to ask anyone.

Everywhere we went, we ran into a lot of people. The men winked at one another as they passed; they would exchange a word or two but never stopped to chat.

We walked through offices that you might have thought belonged to a bank or an insurance company, with everyone sitting at his place, a little plaque in front of him giving his rank and his function. We came to a long hallway on the second floor of the main building. Bob opened a door, and once again it was the right one.

We found ourselves in a very large, well-lit room; the windows were open. No one was there. Beds—five cots and five little cupboards in white wood. On a little table at the head of each bed were large, framed photos of young women. Framed in gold or lacquer. Bob told me they had put up a sixth bed for me. On the bed meant for me I would find three blankets I could wrap myself in when I slept. From one of the cupboards, Bob pulled out three blankets belonging to one of the occupants and showed me how to wrap them around myself to get "perfectly comfortable."

"Handy, isn't it?"

"Yes, Bob."

"OK."

He folded the blankets and put them back. The Signal Corps vehicles were buzzing below.

"And now," said Bob, "let's go to the mess. It's time."

It was close to one in the afternoon.

The mess hall was set up in the school refectory. When we entered, at least a hundred people were already there, and there was no room to sit next to Lieutenant Bradford. Will, who winked at us. We sat down where we could, across from one another, and suddenly Bob got up and motioned for me to get up and follow him. It was to introduce me to some officers, who all seemed very friendly, cordial. One after another, they told me they were very happy to meet me. The colonel also shook my hand, welcoming me.

We sat down again and ate sausage and drank hot chocolate. There were two large pitchers on the table. During the meal, Bob told me he was from Boston and that he worked there as a lawyer. A very interesting and even an agreeable profession, except that it didn't leave him much time to play the violin. He was a great music lover, and some people had told him he would have been even more successful as a professional violinist. But what the heck! Life had decided otherwise. And if his work as a lawyer didn't really leave him much time to play, the war left him even less. None at all. You can't take your violin with you to war, can you? It was a huge deprivation. But things were going well and moving fast. It wasn't going to last much longer. After marching on Berlin with the troops, he was going home.

"You know something," he said, looking at me, his eyes shining, "the day we march on Berlin, I'm going to paint the word *Jude* on my helmet—this big . . ." That was what I'd heard someone else say, the night I met Bill.

After the meal, we parted ways.

"Take it easy!" said Bob. They wouldn't need me until the next morning.

———————

I roamed. I crossed the courtyards. As I approached the gates, I saw a bunch of young people chatting with the soldiers at the front door of one of the buildings. I moved quietly to one side.

The prisoners kept on playing ball behind the barbed wire. I retreated even farther and went to look for Bill over by the cars belonging to the Signal Corps. He wasn't there. I asked where he was.

"Bill? Oh, Bill! He must be in his room."

———————

I found Bill in a room that in ordinary times would have belonged to a dorm monitor. He was organizing his things along with four other young men. Still the same young giant . . .

"Oh, what a nice surprise!" he exclaimed when he saw me. "I didn't know . . ." He gathered all his things into a bundle and threw them into a duffel bag. He shook my hand and said "Oh!" again.

He was quite happy. He had a lot to tell me. Well, had I made up my mind? Had Lieutenants Stone and Bradford managed to convince me? Great! We'd have time to see each other and chat.

He introduced his buddies. One of them was lying on a mattress. He wasn't sleeping. Another was reading. A third was writing. They all told me they were glad to meet me, and they didn't pay us any more attention. The one who was writing put down his pen for a second to shake my hand and then immediately started writing again. Bill told me this guy was always like that; he wrote endlessly, as soon as he had a free moment, pages and pages to his fiancée, with his fiancée's picture in front of him.

Bill said again that he had lots to tell me, unfortunately not right away because he had to go downstairs and be on duty. We'd see each other later. We had time now. In any case, it was just great that I was there. Wow! Really great!

"And you know things are going really well and we'll be in Berlin in a month. Nothing to worry about."

He told me all that as we went down the stairs, after walking through a dorm where there were at least forty guys sleeping on mattresses on the floor.

We passed by on tiptoe. No one moved. He had never seen an armband like the one I was wearing, and could he be so bold as to ask me what it meant?

"Something like the Free French? Oh, I didn't know! Vive de Gaulle! Isn't that what you say? That de Gaulle of yours!"

Bill didn't seem to agree, but it didn't matter to him, he said. Because Bill knew perfectly well what counted and the bishop was right.

"Remember what I told you about our bishop: 'My boys! If you're going over there to keep the world the way it is, then you might as well stay home! But if you're going to change the world, then go!' That bishop, is he ever a great man!"

Bill had heard that with his own ears, and he had thought about it a lot ever since, and the more he thought about it the more he was convinced that the bishop was right.

Definitely! By God, we'd start on it right after the victory.

We parted ways in front of the Signal Corps cars.

I took a walk into town. The streets were full of people, and there were flags everywhere; the weather was still beautiful, and so it was a total surprise when the sky clouded over suddenly and it started to rain. I went into a café to wait. The rain didn't last long, and the sun came out soon after, even more splendid than before.

I went out again and walked along the streets until it was
time to go back to headquarters, and there, just as I was about to enter, the sentry called out and asked me for the password.

Password?

I didn't have a password. Not for a moment had I thought of asking for one; nor had Lieutenant Stone. Which was surprising from such a well-organized man.

I told the sentry that I didn't have a password.

"Who are you?" the sentry asked, scrutinizing me.

I said I was an interpreter.

"Oh, an interpreter?"

"Yes."

Even though I had no password I could mention the names of several people . . . Lieutenant Stone, for example . . .

"Oh, Lieutenant Stone!"

"Lieutenant Bradford."

"Oh, Lieutenant Bradford, too!"

"Yes, of course . . . And Bill from the Signal Corps."

"Bill? OK, you can go."

He gave me a friendly smile. As I passed through, I also mentioned Joe the driver, and at that the sentry burst out laughing and told me it would do fine.

I went in. I went and looked in the courtyard to see whether Joe's jeep was there. It wasn't. I learned that Lieutenants Bradford and Stone had gone off with Joe on a new investigation. No one knew when they'd be back. I walked through the courtyards, smoking my pipe.

There was no one in the prison courtyard behind the

barbed wires except for the military police, who were keeping watch.

Evening arrived, time to go to the mess for dinner. I went. Lieutenants Stone and Bradford still hadn't come back, but the few officers that Lieutenant Stone had introduced me to at lunch greeted me very cordially, and I told one of them the story about the password. He thought it was really funny and started to laugh. Then he told me we weren't supposed to fool around with that sort of thing, especially at night. He gave me the password and suggested that the next day I should ask Lieutenant Stone to give me the daytime password. As I must know, the password changed every day. That was the way it was in every army in the world.

We ate dinner. Sausages, large pitchers of hot chocolate, Nescafé. A very good dinner. Then there was nothing left to do and it was too early to go to bed. All the more so since after the little rainstorm in the afternoon, the weather had gotten nice again and it was going to be a warm evening.

On the other side of the entry gates was a big lawn with a very old oak tree in the middle, and on the lawn, practically underneath the old oak, people were gathered, all sorts of people and all ages, watching the Americans, gossiping, and having a good time. A few soldiers mingled with the crowd. The girls were laughing very loudly. I went and sat on the grass under the oak next to some others who were also sitting quietly, just as people did when there was a party in the village.

After spending quite a while there, I went up to the room. It was empty. But soon after, a tall young lieutenant appeared, thirtyish, with fair, almost white hair, sharp cheekbones and very blue, slightly slanting eyes. He greeted me by name, and I realized that Lieutenant Bob had told him about me.

"Hello, Louis! Glad to meet you!"

He gave me a vigorous handshake. I responded that I was very glad to meet him too, and then he told me his name was

Markov. Lieutenant Markov. Stephan Markov. His friends called him Stef.

After we exchanged these few words, he did a very military half turn and approached his bed. He opened the little white wooden cupboard, took out his uniform jacket and a brush, and began to brush his jacket.

A moment later another lieutenant arrived; he was a little younger than Stef, a tall, fair-haired fellow with glasses, rather fragile looking. He too greeted me by name, and the greeting scene started up again, point by point, while Stef brushed his jacket.

"Glad to meet you," the newcomer said. "My name is Patrick Right."

"Glad to meet you too," I replied.

And with that, he started to undress; he rolled up in his blankets, stretched out on the bed, and closed his eyes immediately.

The third and fourth occupants of the room arrived together, Lieutenants Robert Erikson and Gustavus Wilson.

"Hello Louis . . . My name is Gustavus Wilson. Call me Gus!"

"Hello, Gus! Glad to meet you."

"And I'm Robert Erikson. Call me Bob."

"Hello, Bob! How do you do."

Two more really good guys, you could tell just from looking at them. Bob started writing a letter. Gus went to the window to smoke a last cigarette. Stef, who had finished brushing his jacket, put it back and took his trousers out of the cupboard and started brushing them.

Pat was already snoring quietly.

No one paid any attention to anyone else, and, except for Pat's quiet snoring, all we heard was the scratching of Bob's pen on the paper and, of course, the buzz of the Signal Corps fleet.

I didn't hear the fifth lieutenant arrive. It was time for me to undress and wrap myself up in my three blankets as Lieutenant Stone had demonstrated. Which I did. So I would sleep as soundly as a baby in swaddling clothes. We were much more comfortable rolled up in our three blankets than we would have been in a sleeping bag. All we had to do was close our eyes. And it's true enough that a man who falls asleep closes his eyes to a lot of things . . .

Nights are short in August. When I woke up the next morning, Stef was the only one left in the room. He had his foot on the chair and he was brushing his shoes.

"Good morning, Louis!" he cried, without turning his head. "Sleep well?"

"Good morning, Stef! Slept fine. How about you?"

"Very well, thanks."

Without looking up, he changed feet. Now the other shoe. With two brushes.

I washed up and left.

At the mess hall I found Lieutenant Stone—I mean Bob. We drank a few cups of tea together. He seemed anxious. I mentioned this, and he said it was always that way before a hearing.

"Lousy job!"

The military tribunal was set up in the party room. A little before nine, everyone was in place, even the defendant: a cat. A very young cat, less than twenty. A gracious young cat, surprised, worried, with big shiny eyes, a sad cat standing all alone between two guards from the Military Police armed with rifles. A cat who didn't even dream of taking a leap.

The windows of this large room were open on both sides,

and the morning light came in from everywhere. At the back, behind a long table covered with a green cloth, ten officers were seated. At the center was Lieutenant Colonel Marquez, the presiding judge, a handsome man in the prime of life, very well groomed. His head was rather large, his thick head of hair very black; his face with its regular features wore an expression that might have been boredom. He hung his head at a slight tilt—he seemed to be looking at his fingernails, and when he raised his head, it was to cast his eyes over his surroundings with a certain detachment. His eyes were very blue. His hands remained folded over the papers set out in front of him.

The defendant was sitting on the right side, and not far from him was his defense lawyer, Lieutenant Bradford. On the left was Lieutenant Stone, the prosecutor, pacing back and forth. Also on the left, facing the defendant, a table of stenographers. At the center of the courtroom facing the judges was a chair for the witnesses. Lieutenant Stone asked me to stand next to it.

No one uttered a word until it turned nine.

All you could hear was the now familiar buzz of the Signal Corps cars, the passing of a squadron of planes, and a few bombs going off near Brest.

———

At nine o'clock sharp, Lieutenant Colonel Marquez declared the court in session and gave the floor to Lieutenant Stone. The stenographers bent over their machines—a newfangled kind, absolutely noiseless.

Lieutenant Stone, who couldn't stand still, repeated the story of that terrible evening. Pacing back and forth, approaching the bench and then moving away, and getting more and more animated as he spoke, he told all, from the young girl's visit to the base to the sound of the defendant's footsteps in the courtyard of the farm as night fell—the light they put out, the mother and father pushing against the door, the hatchet they couldn't find, and finally the gunshot.

"Nothing can excuse such a dreadful, cowardly act; there is not the shadow of an extenuating circumstance; everyone is already convinced, beginning with the defendant himself, who, you should know, has made a complete confession and pleads guilty . . ."

Everyone listened in total silence. Nothing was moving anywhere except the stenographers' fingers.

Lieutenant Colonel Marquez, his hands folded over the papers in front of him, still seemed to be looking at his fingernails. At the end of his speech, Lieutenant Stone took a tiny object, shining like a jewel, out of his pocket and raised it in front of everyone in a quasi-liturgical gesture. Holding the jewel between his thumb and his index finger, raising high his elegant violinist's hand, he walked the whole length of the table, taking small steps so that all the officers could see it clearly.

"Here is the bullet!"

The defendant, still standing all alone and more motionless than anyone else, was the same cat with terrified eyes— the only black man in this assembly of whites.

Lieutenant Stone put the bullet back into his pocket and stopped speaking. He let the silence continue; then he asked the presiding judge to bring in the witnesses.

His hands still folded over his papers, his head bent, Lieutenant Colonel Marquez looked up.

"Would you please ask the interpreter to raise his right hand?"

Lieutenant Stone turned toward me. He asked me to raise my right hand.

I raised my right hand.

"Please ask the interpreter," Lieutenant Marquez continued, "to swear to translate truthfully the questions of the court to the witnesses and the answers of those witnesses to the court."

"Do you swear," Lieutenant Stone asked me, "to translate according to the truth the questions of the court to the witnesses and the responses of the witnesses to the court? Say: 'I so swear.'"

"I so swear."

"Good. Bring in the first witness," he ordered one of the men from the Military Police. The man went out and came back with the young girl's mother. He led her to the chair. She sat down; I remained standing next to her. The man from the Military Police left.

In profound silence all eyes turned toward this woman dressed in black, with the torn cheek, who was looking straight in front of her with her hands in her lap.

"Would you please administer the oath to the witness?" Lieutenant Colonel Marquez asked Lieutenant Stone, who transmitted the question to me.

I translated the question for the mother. She rose. She raised her right hand. She swore to tell the truth. Lieutenant Stone asked her to be seated. Then he turned to me.

"And now, ask the witness to tell us, in her own words . . ."

Just as she had done in her own home, with the same calm voice, the same slow and even delivery, she started telling the story of that horrendous evening once again. She told how they had heard steps in the courtyard and thought it was a neighbor, how the young girl had opened the window and caught sight of a soldier, how she had closed the window hastily and turned out the light, and how the father had locked the door. She talked about the kicking at the door, the door being hit by the rifle butt, the hatchet that the young girl hadn't found, and finally the bullet fired at the door and her husband collapsing at her feet, half of his skull blown off. Then she fell silent. She had nothing to add. There were no further questions. She could be dismissed. The order was given by the presiding judge.

The man from the Military Police led her out. Then he returned with the girl, who was also asked to raise her right hand and tell the truth, the whole truth, and nothing but the truth. She took the oath. Lieutenant Stone turned to me:

"And now ask the witness to say in her own words . . ."

The girl told the same story as her mother. Next, the presiding judge had Lieutenant Stone ask her questions.

"Ask the witness . . ."

He wanted to know whether the girl had spoken to the black soldier when she had gone to the base.

"No."

"So, you didn't know him?"

Were they trying to imply that perhaps she had made a date with him? That she had invited him?

"No no, oh no!" she cried out, blushing, horrified.

And now, ask the witness if, in her opinion, the young soldier was drunk?

"No," she replied.

Then she thought. She said she didn't know.

"That's fine. You are dismissed."

The stenographers took the opportunity to rest for a moment before Lieutenant Bradford began the defense. All the stenographers' hands rose at the same time and rested on the machines, and as soon as the presiding judge announced that the defense had the floor, every hand came back down over the keys.

––––––––

Lieutenant Bradford's argument was brief. He didn't try to deny the horror of the facts or to invent any extenuating circumstances. He entered a guilty plea and let the court know that the murderer deeply regretted his act. The information gathered about him showed him to be a good, honest boy up to the present, though from very modest origins.

As awful as it was, the terrible thing of which he was accused was simply an accident. He was not an assassin, he had premeditated none of it. Furthermore we were dealing with a young life of twenty years. Men of conscience, free men, citizens of a great democracy must think twice before sending this hugely irresponsible young man to the gallows. Certainly he deserved punishment, but let this punishment be imprisonment for as long as they liked. Spare him the noose!

By sparing his life, give him a chance to redeem himself. Lieutenant Bradford had interviewed the defendant at great length in his prison cell and he could assure the court that the work of repentance had already begun. We must not interfere with God's work on a human soul!

––––––––––

The court adjourned for deliberations. With nothing more to do there, I left, crossed the courtyard and went out into the street. I wandered around.

Someone called out to me. I found myself face to face with a young FFI in combat uniform: his helmet was covered in green mosquito netting. He told me his name.

We had met one another before in meetings.

I remembered: he was a schoolteacher.

He asked me what I was doing there.

I told him, and said I had just come from a court-martial where they were trying a black soldier. He asked me if I enjoyed doing that. I said I didn't. And I asked him what *he* was doing there. He answered that he was embarrassed because he had lost his unit. He didn't know how to get back to them.

I brought him back to headquarters and took him straight to the Signal Corps, where I hoped to find Bill. He wasn't there. He was sleeping: he'd been on duty all night. I dealt with someone else.

We explained. It didn't take him long to get us the coordinates that would allow the FFI to find his unit. An officer arrived. He asked what this was about. We told him. The officer asked if the FFI had eaten.

"No? Take him to the mess hall. After he's eaten, we'll find him a car to help him get back."

I took the FFI to the mess hall, left him there, and went back to the garages. I wanted to see if Joe's car was there. It was, and so was Joe.

It was Joe who told me the verdict: he was to be hanged by the neck until he was dead. Lieutenant Stone had just told Joe himself. For that matter, Lieutenant Stone was looking for me everywhere, Joe said, to take the witnesses to the treasury officer. He, Joe, would drive them back home to their hamlet.

I went to look for Lieutenant Stone, but it was he who caught up with me.

"Did you see? I was trembling like a leaf when I showed the bullet. Yes indeed, like a leaf."

He wasn't in favor of the death penalty, anymore than Lieutenant Bradford was. But what could you do?

"Lieutenant Bradford is a man of convictions. So am I. In his view, as in mine, a life is a life, even the life of one of those little Harlem blacks, however guilty he might be. And believe me, Louis, I am not a racist. Not at all. I'm Jewish, you know! But then again, what can you do? And did you see that poor woman with her cheek . . ."

Lieutenant Bradford had gone to see the condemned man in his prison cell. It was true that the repentance of the condemned man was total and sincere—we mustn't think that Lieutenant Bradford was trying to manipulate the court.

If there was any hope, though Lieutenant Stone didn't

think there was, it was up to a board of review, after studying the trial transcript.

Anyway!

Now, if I would be kind enough to take the two women to the treasury officer?

They had gone to their hotel but would be back any moment. The treasury officer would give them their pay and Joe would take them home. That would be all for me for today. Unless some investigation came up unexpectedly.

"Take it easy!"

————

I found my young FFI again, leaving the mess hall. They'd served him a meal. But what he was happiest about was the welcome he'd gotten. Starting with the way they'd welcomed him at the Signal Corps.

"Would you have believed it, would you? Immediate trust. It's incredible. No one's going to believe me. And they're giving me a car! These people are extraordinary—they're a great example for us—not to mention all we owe them for liberating us. They're going to accomplish great things, I'm sure of it . . ."

At the mess hall, all the people he'd met were so friendly!

"Are they always that way?"

"From what I've seen so far, yes."

"Are you going to stay with them?"

I'd rather not be asked that question. I didn't feel right in the court-martial.

"What did they sentence him to?"

"Hanging."

I saw him shudder.

"I've always been opposed to the death sentence," he started in again. "We were fighting this war against capital punishment too. What about you, do you think there's going to be a third world war?"

He had met people who believed it, who proclaimed it, who said it was inevitable. Between Russia and America.

"When this one isn't even over!"

He put out his hand to shake mine at the same time as he was responding to a GI, a colleague of Joe's, who was waving to him as he stood by a car, waiting for him.

Just then the two women crossed the courtyard, the mother holding her little bundle of belongings. At the sight of the mother's wounded cheek he put his hand up to his own cheek as if to reassure himself that it was intact.

"What did he do, the man they condemned?"

"Killed the husband and father of these two women."

"How?"

"By firing at the door."

He shrugged. Then he ran off, clutching his gun with his hand on the butt to keep it from rattling.

The prison courtyard was deserted except for two men from the Military Police who were standing guard at the barbed wire.

I took the two women to the treasurer's office. They had the mother sign various papers and gave her a few hundred francs as compensation for her testimony and that of her daughter. Everything was in order; nothing left to do but go to the garages.

Joe was there, calm and patient as always, smoking a cigarette as he waited and smiling amiably when he saw the two women approach. The mother held the money they'd just given her in her hand. She looked as though she didn't know where to put it.

Before getting into the car, she gave it to her daughter and asked her to put it in her purse. The girl took the money, put it in her purse. They got into the car; Joe sat down behind the wheel. We exchanged a few words of farewell and didn't make the slightest allusion to what had just happened, that is, to the verdict.

Joe was about to shift into gear when a man came running up; he'd come from the kitchens carrying a whole armful of boxes and packages, boxes of rice, coffee, all kinds of canned goods, rations, cartons of cigarettes, candy, chewing gum, sugar: gifts that the man spread joyfully on the two women's laps, saying "Santa Claus!"

"What is he saying?" the young girl asked me.

"Père Noël!"

The two women, dumbfounded, didn't know how to respond. They stared at the packages. The man withdrew, saluting very militarily.

The car started. OK, Joe!

I watched the jeep go through the gates, and I left, lighting my pipe.

The day passed that way, and then it was time for dinner at the mess hall. I didn't run into either Lieutenant Stone or Lieutenant Bradford there. I sat down in the first empty seat I spotted. People were very pleasant; no one asked me any questions about who I was or what I was doing there. We winked at one another and when the meal ended, everyone went his own way.

As I left I passed the kitchens and saw heaps of food, especially pastries, which the flies and yellow jackets were assailing, and I thought it was leftovers about to be thrown away. I asked a passerby if all that was really going into the trash? He burst out laughing. Of course it was all going to be thrown away. Leftovers? No. Surplus. It was the same every day.

I was reluctant to tell him that it was very regrettable, there was enough there to feed at least twenty poor families. I told him anyway, and he started to laugh again.

"That may be," he answered. But what I was asking for was against regulations. And what about sanitary precautions? He walked away laughing. I thought I would go back up to bed and take a nap. I had eaten too much; the food was too good and I wasn't used to it. But I ran into Bill. He tagged along. He had a ton of things to tell me.

––––––––

As an inquisitive person, a responsible person, Bill keeps a "war diary." I was the first person he had met since he'd been in France that he wanted to chat with.

We went into his room. Everything was as before: the sleeping man stretched out on a mattress; the reader sitting on a chair with his feet propped up on the edge of a table; and, in the back, the one who was writing to his fiancée.

We said hello; that is, we exchanged smiles and winks. Bill offered me a chair, rummaged in his bag and pulled out a big notebook, which he opened and set on a table. He showed me the first page of the notebook on which, in capital letters, he had transcribed the bishop's words: "My boys . . . if it's to keep the world the way it is . . . but if it's to change it . . ."

Bill stood looking at me for a good long moment, pointing at the sentence with his index finger, his baby face shining. "How about that for deep meaning!"

He sat down. He flipped through the notebook. Maybe he wanted to read me one or two passages, but he was hesitating. Finally he took out a pad of paper. To take notes. He asked my age. I told him I was forty-four. He noted it down. Then he sat with his pencil poised, and finally he asked me what it was like during all those years of occupation. I told him it wasn't very easy to answer a question like that off the top of my head.

He was ready to admit that. It was all still too fresh, all of that—he understood quite well, we didn't have enough perspective, but he could tell me, in the meantime, that the propaganda from London had had some unfortunate effects on the American public and that, for example, one of the great surprises for the Americans, after they'd landed in France, had been to find people more or less well clothed, however shabbily, and more or less nourished, however badly. They were expecting much worse.

"I'd like you to tell me what happened to you personally."

60
∀ I wanted to tell him that he was very young and that I myself felt very old. Since he insisted and since he was desperate for at least one memory and since he was so friendly, I told him that the best I could do for a young citizen of a great democracy whose mascot is a Statue of Liberty would be to tell him how, one spring morning, I was pushed into the street by a German soldier.

It must have been around ten o'clock. We were walking in opposite directions on the street edge of the sidewalk. I didn't give him any space. Shoving me with his shoulder, he pushed me into the street. We turned toward each other. He gave me a threatening look. I walked away.

"Would you have liked to deal with that, Bill?"

In a very low voice he answered, "No."

"Another time, Bill, at night . . ."

I started telling him the story, though I had no real desire to. How to make Bill understand what it was like to walk through your own city in the darkest night without finding the way except by groping at the walls. It was long past curfew, and there was no moon. It was December. That night I had to take a message to Christian at the other end of town. Having accomplished my mission, I was returning along streets that were darker than ever, finding my way only by feeling the stones on the houses. I came to what I knew was an intersection. There, wrapped in the kind of silence you only get in the depths of the countryside, I heard steps. I stopped at a door and stopped moving. It wasn't the patrol; it was the steps of one man but he was wearing boots. I waited. The footsteps stopped. I started walking. I heard the footsteps again. Then I realized that the man who, like me, was walking in the dark had heard mine. He sought me out. We found ourselves face to face, so close to each other that in spite of the darkness I could tell something about his face—especially his eyes; they were the face, the eyes, of a very young German soldier. A soldier on furlough. He had come from Russia. And since it was Christmas, he'd love to find a place with a bit of light and some people to celebrate the holiday with. He'd gotten lost. What to do? I told him he should try to find the train station. His people would be there. But the train station, how to find the train station? I told him to walk straight ahead. He might run into his patrol. He held out his hand, saying, "Bon Noël . . . Joyeux Noël." I answered by wishing him a merry Christmas in turn, and we each went our own way.

"So you see, Bill . . ."

"I see . . . Have you kept a war diary?"

At that point Lieutenant Stone arrived, as lively as ever and exclaiming good-naturedly that having looked all over and not finding me anywhere, it occurred to him that I could only be with Bill.

"And how right I was! Come along. I've got important news for you. You're not too mad at me for taking away our interpreter, are you Bill?"

Bill wasn't too mad, just a little; he said he really hoped we'd see each again before long, wistfully putting his war diary back into his bag.

Lieutenant Stone (I still can't bring myself to say Bob) didn't tell me right away where he was taking me; he first wanted to explain why I hadn't found him in the mess hall.

It was because just as he and Lieutenant Bradford were getting ready to go, they'd been summoned for a new investigation, a nasty affair of the same type as the first and maybe even worse.

As for the news concerning me, it was that, given my excellent services, he'd asked the colonel that I be officially attached to headquarters. The colonel had agreed, and so we were heading straight to his office to fill out the official papers. Then Bob would take me to the uniform supply room, where I would be given a complete outfit.

In my capacity as official interpreter-translator, I would be given the rank of lieutenant and would be paid. Then we would move on to the kitchen, where I could choose what I wanted to have made up as packages that I could send to my family and friends.

"Is that all right?"

––––––––––

The colonel received us with great courtesy. He was at his desk. He stood up to greet us and had us sit down before sitting down again himself; he was a man in his fifties with completely white hair, very elegant, urbane, with pale pink skin and blue eyes. Smiling.

Good! The papers were in order. It was all set. He didn't need to repeat what I already knew from Lieutenant Stone, did he, but he could thank me personally for the fine service I had already provided to the army. As a matter of fact, the papers he was giving me would be especially useful in dealing with the Military Police. You had to be wary of those people. Sometimes they were overeager about doing their job, and they could be quick on the trigger.

"Well, good luck! Do you also speak German? Not very well? But well enough? Good! You'll come with us to Germany. We're going to bring your prisoners home!"

He rose and accompanied us to the door. We shook hands cordially. The interview had lasted three minutes.

I was surprised that the colonel hadn't asked me who I was.
No one had ever asked me, not even Lieutenant Stone or Lieutenant Bradford.

Before going to the uniform supply room, Bob wanted to stop
at the mess hall. He hadn't had breakfast and he needed a nice
cup of tea and some pastries.
"You'll surely have a cup of tea with me? Yes. Naturally.
Why not? And the colonel's a very decent guy too, couldn't
you tell?"

"Yes. I could tell."

At the mess hall we were served by a very young guy,
skinny, red-haired, and freckled. Bob pointed out that this
kid was kind of a thug but not stupid, and quite friendly, with
just the right touch of insolence.

"What's good about the army is that you meet all kinds
of people, every kind. On the one hand, your friend Bill, for
instance, and here, this little thug. Bill's a great kid, a very good
character. Did he talk to you about his bishop?

"Yes."

"Of course. He was very impressed by the bishop's speech.
Good!"

He emptied his cup, and we left for the uniform supply
room.

How the devil does he manage to show interest in so many
things of no interest whatever, moving from one to the other,
never changing?

Lieutenant Stone is an intelligent man, refined, cultivated,
distinguished-looking—a middle-class bachelor in his forties,
very good-natured, a really decent guy and a good democrat,
a good Jew, passionate about music: as he walked, he started

to hum a tune from *La Bohème*, and then suddenly stopped humming and paused in the middle of the corridor we were walking down to tell me about his violin.

Every day for years he had practiced his violin, and now it had been months since he had been able to . . . Would he ever get his technique back? How to make up for lost time? How to get back to that level of virtuosity—he might as well say it—that had cost him so much hard work?

With his beautiful hand he pretended to draw his bow over the chords of a violin, then he sighed, "Let's just hope I do!"

Still as sure of the way as if he thought he could find it with his eyes closed, Bob led me through new labyrinths until we reached a courtyard containing a long, low wooden hut, an Adriant barrack,* in which, all alone, surrounded by his supplies, which were piled up on shelves, we found a very tall sergeant, thin and sad-looking. Bob explained things briefly.

"Do you understand, sergeant? A complete outfit. We're talking about an official interpreter!"

"OK," the sergeant answered morosely, without the slightest crease appearing on his face, as if he were afraid that when he spoke, his long cheeks, white and stiff as plaster, might crack.

"Fix him up!" Bob called out to him as he turned around to leave.

But first he alerted me that he'd be back in no time to help me carry my package up to my bed.

As soon as Bob had left, the sergeant studied me silently from head to toe. He sized me up; I watched his eyes move all over me, and I guessed by the furrow in his brow that he was measuring. Finally he moved toward the shelves, took down all sorts of clothes, carried them in a pile to a long table, like a counter, made of planks and set on stilts, and threw them

*A prefabricated barrack built during WWI.

down. He went to the back of the hut for a pair of boots, which he placed on the pile. He went to one shelf and took down a cap; and just as I was wondering, looking at this pile, if I shouldn't start trying things on, he decided to tell me that all I had to do now was carry the gear to my room, and that if something didn't fit I could just come back. In his opinion, everything ought to fit because he had looked me over carefully.

I attached the boots to each other by their laces and hung them around my neck; then I took the whole load and left without waiting for Bob to come back.

I hadn't gone three steps when Bob arrived. Seeing me up to my neck with the load, he laughed heartily and announced there was still something missing from my equipment but that he had thought of it.

"Take a look!" he cried, pulling a small piece of cloth out of his pocket and shaking it open like a handkerchief, still laughing. "It's an armband! It's meant to show the whole world your status as a Volontary Free Frenchman with the American troops. You can wear it on your left sleeve instead of that FN armband, which you can put in your pocket. Wait a minute! Give me half of all that stuff! How can you expect to make it to your room all by yourself with all that gear? You can't see your own feet."

Once in the room, the packages thrown on my bed, Bob left. I sat on the next bed and felt like smoking a pipe. Despite my desire, I didn't.

The windows in the room were wide open; the sun was shining brightly. There must have been a garden out there; birds were chirping. There was so much chirping that at times I could barely hear the buzz of the Signal Corps cars. On a little table at the head of the bed I was sitting on was a color photo of a very elegant, very pretty young woman. A long, delicate face with big blue eyes ready to smile.

I don't know how long I stayed there listening to the birds and looking at the photo, or how I decided to take off my old clothes and put on the new ones. It happened very quickly. Everything fit perfectly. The sergeant knew his job! I put on the boots. You'd have thought they were made to order for me. I took a few steps to make sure. They were perfect.

I felt rich in my new uniform, solid, comfortable, except that I also felt slightly ashamed, almost as if I had stolen it all.

I bundled my old clothes and shoved them into the cupboard. Then I lay down on my bed and fell asleep.

———

I must have slept soundly because I didn't hear the others come back, or else they must have been very quiet. They were all there when Joe came to wake me, all four of them—Stef Markov, Patrick Right, Robert Erikson, Gustavus Wilson. Of the four, three were already lying down and two were asleep.

The one who wasn't sleeping was Sergeant Gus Wilson, and the one who was still up was Lieutenant Patrick Right. They asked me if I had slept well, and I told them I had. Soundly and for quite a long time, for I noticed they had closed the windows and it was already dark. The only light came from a weak blue bulb on the ceiling. Joe bent over me, his hand on my shoulder, and shook me gently. The lieutenants were waiting for me downstairs. We were about to leave on a mission. I got up and followed Joe across the barely lit hallways. It was dark in the courtyard. In the middle of the courtyard stood the jeep, and next to the jeep several shadows: Lieutenants Stone and Bradford; a man from the Military Police, helmeted and armed; and a fourth shadow, that of a smallish soldier, whom they ordered into the backseat. The MP climbed in next to him. We had to squeeze into what space was left, Lieutenant

Bradford on one side, next to the MP, me on the other. Bob got in next to Joe.

"OK, Joe," said Bob, once he was seated.

Joe shifted into gear, and we took off at a good speed as soon as we'd passed through the gates. We soon found ourselves out in the country. I realized I probably wasn't fully awake when I had to have Bob repeat the question he had just asked me: "How does it feel to be in uniform?"

I said it felt very good. The sergeant in charge of the supplies really knew his job: "Yes, I do feel good, Bob, but a bit silly."

Lieutenant Bradford said that everyone feels a bit like that at first, even in civilian life when you leave the tailor's in a custom-made suit. To which Bob added that it's like that, too, when you get home from the barber's.

"And did you remember to put on your armband?"

No. I hadn't thought of it. Bob advised me to do so by the next day, adding that it was very important, especially because of the MPs.

I glanced at the MP and was flabbergasted when I realized that the man sitting next to him was a young black soldier just like the one they had tried that morning. Compared to him, the MP with his carbine lying straight across his knee looked like a giant.

I didn't say another word. Neither did the others.

We drove for a long time, crossing deserted villages where everything was shut, without a glimmer of light. The farther we went, the darker the night became, but Joe kept driving at the same speed with the same confidence.

We left the main road and went down a lane. Bob seemed to be dozing off. A bump in the road woke him, and at the same time, the MP dropped his carbine, which fell with a loud clang. He retrieved it. Lieutenant Bradford, sitting up straight, his hands folded over his stomach, was lost in thought.

In the shadows I saw the gleam of the little black soldier's eyes. Bob grunted. He muttered something incomprehensible, probably a complaint about what a hell of a job this was. That's what I thought I heard, but he didn't repeat himself. We drove still farther, and finally the car stopped in a deep, narrow lane. We had arrived.

No one moved right away. Joe leaned over the car door, wide-eyed, scouring the night. This was the place all right. Bob got out first. He took a few steps in the darkness, then returned to the car. I got out next, and we took off together down the narrow pathway. Bob held out his flashlight. He flashed it, and we could make out a small house in a clearing.

He told me it was what we were looking for and that we'd go up to the house and wake the inhabitants. We went up. Bob knocked at the door but no one answered. His knocks resonated loudly in the night. He knocked harder and still no one answered. The house seemed dead. Not a crack of light anywhere.

"They're afraid," Bob told me as he started to pound again.

He aimed his flashlight at the front of the house. We saw that all the shutters were closed. He asked me to call out, and I was about to when a shutter on the first floor creaked. The lieutenant immediately turned on his flashlight again and aimed it at the window.

In the cone of light the face of a young man appeared.

"Tell him who we are. Tell him we need everyone in the house to come down and that there's nothing to be afraid of."

I told the young man, but he wasn't convinced.

"At this hour?" he replied.

"Tell him we've come to investigate."

The young man disappeared, closing the shutters.

We waited. Then there was the squeaking of a lock, the clink of a chain removed, and the door opened. The young man had a flashlight too. He turned it on and pointed it at us.

"Oh, good! If that's it . . ."

He opened, we entered. He closed the door again, turning off the flashlight at the same time as he turned on the light in the room. There were four or five people there, including two women and an old man.

"Tell them we've brought him."

I translated. They didn't budge.

"Tell them I'd like them to come with us down to the lane."

I translated. They refused.

"Insist. We need their testimony. They have to come."

I translated; they took a long time answering, then one of the women said, "We have to go."

We all went back to the car.

When he heard us arrive, the MP made the black soldier get out of the car. Lieutenant Bradford got out. Joe stayed at the wheel. I saw him light a cigarette.

We led the black soldier out and stood him in front of the car. Bob arranged the people from the house in a half-circle in front of him, then stationed himself to the left of the black soldier, with Lieutenant Bradford on his right. The MP stood at a slight distance, his carbine under his arm.

The lieutenants turned on their flashlights and pointed them at the face of the soldier, who was smaller than they. Standing at attention, he didn't budge. There was a profound silence; all you could hear was the rustling of wind in the leaves.

Beneath the crossed flashlights, his motionless face with its copper and bronze hues, his big white eyes not looking at anyone, made him look like an idol.

"Do you recognize this man?"

No one answered right away. Then we heard "Yes."

"Yes. It's him . . ."

One after another they said and repeated that he was the one. The lieutenants turned off their flashlights and the MP drew nearer. The people went home. We got back into the car.

"OK, Joe!"

Before he shifted into gear, Joe threw out his cigarette.

———————

We drove home. No one uttered a word until we arrived at headquarters. As we were parting, Bob reminded me that I had to be in court the next morning at nine o'clock.

I don't know how I found my room, it was as black as outdoors, or how I found my bed. I fell asleep right away, wrapped in my three blankets.

Yes, it's true that a man who falls asleep closes his eyes to a lot of things . . .

———————

It was already broad daylight when I awoke. No one was left in the room but Stef Markov. Hunched over with his foot on the chair, Stef was brushing his shoes.

"Hello, Louis," he called out. "Sleep well?"

"Hello, Stef! I slept well, thanks. How about you?"

"Thanks. Very well."

"Nice weather, huh?"

"Sure is!"

The room was full of sunlight.

He shifted feet. Now the other shoe. With two brushes. When he was finished, he arranged his instruments—brushes, tubes, rags—in a box, which he put back into his cupboard; he took a jacket out of the cupboard and picked up another brush to brush the jacket. He put back the jacket and the brush, closed the cupboard, glanced at his bed to make sure everything was tidy, and left.

"Good-bye, Louis. See you soon."

"See you soon, Stef."

I got up, washed up, and left. It certainly was a beautiful day. Going downstairs, I realized I had forgotten my armband, and I went back up to the room. I found the armband in my cupboard. I tried to put it on but couldn't. I shoved the armband into my pocket and left for the mess hall, where I heard talk about the action taking place outside Brest.

A little before nine o'clock I went up to the courtroom and found everyone where they belonged, the officers sitting on either side of Lieutenant Colonel Marquez behind the long table covered with a green cloth; then Bob, standing to the left of the courtroom, and Lieutenant Bradford standing to the right. Everyone was at their post, including the stenographers seated behind their machines, and the defendant, between two MPs.

It was another black man, not the one we had taken out the night before, but a different one, a tall young man, very muscular, very handsome, who stood at attention without looking at anyone, without looking anywhere.

At nine o'clock sharp the trial began, and Lieutenant Colonel Marquez gave the floor to Bob.

As soon as Bob started speaking, it was clear that it was a case of rape or attempted rape. The defendant pleaded guilty. A woman had been forcibly dragged into the bushes.

We were about to hear her testimony. She was the principal witness.

An MP went to fetch her. Bob led the young woman toward the chair I was standing next to. They had her swear to tell the truth, the whole truth, and nothing but the truth. She raised her right hand and swore. They asked me to swear to translate the witness's deposition faithfully. Then Bob turned to me again, wagged his index finger with the severity of a man conscious of the importance of what was about to happen, and said:

"And now, ask the witness to tell in her own words . . ."

I translated.

The young woman told how she was going on an errand in the village when she met the black soldier, who approached her in a very friendly way and spoke to her at first with a smile, then grabbed her by the arm. She struggled. He forced her into the bushes and raped her there.

"He raped me."

I translated.

Immediately, Lieutenant Colonel Marquez raised his head (he'd been looking at his fingernails).

"No," he said. "The witness can't say that. That word can't be part of the testimony. It is up to the court to determine whether or not a rape has taken place."

He turned to Bob.

"Ask the witness precise questions."

Bob took a deep breath. I saw his face tense up with effort. Finally he said, "Ask the witness: Did he put his private parts into her private parts?"

He let his arms go lax as though he were thinking, "There, that's it, I actually said it . . ."

I translated.

The young woman didn't answer immediately. In the silence that followed, everyone held their breath. Between a yes and a no: the noose. Did she know? Did she want them to hang him? No one had informed her of the consequences of her response. No one who would have been qualified.

The defendant remained as motionless and silent as he had been since the beginning. The young woman answered, "Yes."

———

I spent the rest of the day doing nothing but wander around the courtyard and the buildings after taking the young woman to the treasury officer, where she was given her witness's pay. We didn't exchange two words.

As she was getting into the car that was going to take her home, she was given presents—cartons of cigarettes, candy, and so forth. She didn't even smile as she took them. The car started up. I went on my way. It was already late in the morning. I felt like going into town. I noticed Bill and made sure he didn't see me, but right after that I ran into Bob, who wagged his finger at me as soon as he caught sight of me.

"What about that armband? You forgot to put your armband on your sleeve, Mr. Official Interpreter!"

I took the armband out of my pocket. Bob put it on my left sleeve himself, which amused him no end. A man passed by and stared at us, intrigued, until Bob lost his temper and shouted, "He is an official interpreter, Private!"

The soldier fled, and Bob turned to me all smiles; he managed to fasten the armband by making a knot, and then he stood back to see how it looked on my sleeve. He seemed to approve, and finally said,

"Now, take it easy!"

He was about to leave, but I could tell from his eyes that he still had something to say. I too had something to ask. What was the verdict? But we didn't say anything, either of us. We knew full well what it was.

Bob twirled around and went off, repeating, "Take it easy!"

————

The next day there was no hearing. Bob and I took the opportunity to make a trip into town. We spent almost an hour in the fish market, then in the shops. Bob wanted to buy souvenirs to take back to the States. We didn't find much. He particularly wanted some bottles of fancy French perfume. We couldn't find any.

In the afternoon Lieutenant Bradford, Bob, and I left in the car, driven as usual by Joe. There was a new investigation. We spoke to some people in a village, but it became clear that the investigation didn't have much of a foundation. The lieutenants decided to give up on it.

On our way home, I learned from one of Bob's questions to Lieutenant Bradford that Bradford's wife had just given birth.

It was still very early when we got back. As he left us, Bob warned me to be ready for the hearing the next morning, at nine o'clock.

When I arrived at the hearing the next morning, I saw that the defendant was another black man.

The court-martial went much like the earlier ones; everything was carefully recorded by the stenographers. The defendant pleaded guilty. He never said a word. Just like his predecessors, he remained impassive from beginning to end. He too had tried to rape a woman. The court was adjourned. The MPs escorted the defendant out. Everyone scattered, lighting cigarettes.

It was through Bob, a little later, that I learned that the defendant had been condemned to a number of years in prison and that the very polite colonel who had received me as a social equal and had given me the papers guaranteeing my status as an official interpreter had thrown a fit of anger when he learned the verdict. He had even railed quite crudely against the members of the court who didn't have the balls to pronounce a death sentence.

The battle for Brest continues day after day; no one has any doubts about the outcome. As soon as the German general and his forty thousand men surrender, we will leave for Germany.

Except for planes flying overhead and bombs exploding, what we heard of the battle was hard to fathom, although once, when an explosion of such violence resounded in the middle of an afternoon, we assumed that the Germans were blowing up their installations and it was all over. We were wrong.

More days passed, the military court was in session nearly every morning, and every time the defendant was a black man and the accusation was the same.

There were also times when several defendants were tried at once, and all of them were black. One morning, there were four of them. They didn't say a word. Why were they silent like that, why did they all plead guilty? Eventually I asked Bob.

"Because they are!" he answered, throwing up his hands as if to show his surprise at such a question. As if I thought it wasn't a matter of simple evidence. Guilty. They in fact were. They admitted it themselves.

"But why always blacks, Bob?"

"Ah! That's a hell of a problem!"

"I know, Bob. Apparently you have to be an American to understand it. But why only blacks? It isn't a special tribunal for blacks?"

He grew almost indignant. How could I think of such a thing? A special tribunal? Of course not! Did I really think he or any other members of the court liked having only black men to try?

"It's certainly not our fault if they can't even look at a woman without trying to rape her."

One morning at the hearing—and again it was a black man being tried——the witnesses were about to be introduced when the presiding judge, Lieutenant Colonel Marquez, ordered four black soldiers to be brought in from the prison and lined up on either side of the defendant.

Four black soldiers arrived, escorted by MPs. The five blacks were ordered to stand up straight in a row. The first witness, a farmer, was introduced. The other witnesses waited their turn in an adjacent room. The first witness was asked to approach the five black soldiers and put his hand on the shoulder of the one he thought was guilty.

The first witness stepped forward, walked straight to the defendant, and put his large hand on the man's shoulder, looking just like a farmer about to close a deal. The defendant didn't even quiver. The witness returned to his place. That would be all.

"Bring in the second witness!"

The second witness didn't hesitate either; he put his hand on the defendant's shoulder, then turned around and went back to his place.

"The third witness . . ."

The fourth witness, then the fifth, stepped forward in turn. As the scene unfolded, the silence grew more and more oppressive. Even Bob looked undone.

What I missed the most during those days, aside from a few people, was the evening walk I used to take when I was still at home, the few moments I spent on my bench at the rotary, that walk across the bridge, where I used to stop for a few moments to look at the poplars that lined the stream at the bottom of the valley, listening to the sound of the water as it ran over the pebbles. No matter how many free hours I had to wander wherever I wanted ("Take it easy!"), they were never the right hours.

On some evenings I would go and sit under the tall oak tree in front of the school gates. There were always a lot of people there, especially young men and women who laughed and chatted with the American soldiers until night fell. At other times I went to look for Bill in his room when he wasn't on duty. He was studying law and keeping his war diary up to date, always surrounded by the same roommates, one busy writing to his fiancée, the other reading, the third stretched out on his mattress.

When I got there, we always winked and smiled at each other. I wondered if Bill was going to tell me about his bishop again. He practically always did, but now there was something else on his mind.

They were going to change the world, there was no doubt about it, but that might not be as easy as he had thought. Victory was near, that was for sure. Patton was advancing, so were the Russians . . . But that was the point! What would happen when the Russians got to Berlin? Before changing the world and in order to change it, wouldn't they have to put an end to communism first? Wouldn't they?

"Don't you have a lot of armed communists in France? What are they called? The FTP?"

Bill had read something about that in the newspaper. He was beginning to think that the cost of changing the world would be a third world war.

"And how many political parties do you have in France? We only have two. Because we are a true democracy."

"Tell me, Bill," I asked him one night, "why are they only trying black men here?"

"Oh! You don't understand them. They're out of control!"

He didn't like to talk about it. He didn't like the subject.

"Those people don't know how to act. They are incapable of self-discipline. Before *I* left for Europe, I promised my mother not to drink a drop of alcohol and not to go near any girls. I'll stay true to my word, you can believe that!"

I answered that I had no trouble believing him. I even told him that he was right and that things like that weren't meant for a decent young man like him. But that didn't help me understand, I told him, why only black men were being tried here and why another one was to be tried the next morning—and why, without a doubt, he would be sentenced to hang.

––––––––––

Incidentally, where were they hanged? And who was the hangman? It probably took place at dawn, as everywhere in the world where people are hanged, where people are executed, where heads are cut off. People were still sleeping at that hour—myself along with the others, wrapped warmly in my three blankets, surrounded by my roommates, Stef, Pat, Robert, and Gus, also sleeping soundly. No one ever knew. The thing was long done by the time we opened our eyes.

I'd watch Stef Markov run to the sink and wash himself thoroughly, shave, return to his bed, and brush his clothes, shine his shoes. Stef always seemed to be getting ready to go to some fancy reception. I'd see another one of them opening the window to check the weather, and the first words I'd hear would be that the day was going to be as beautiful as the one before; the splendid summer was always the same, continuing day after day, the same enchanting light, and yet there was that rope, and at the end of that rope a child of the shadows, his body gone limp. And tomorrow, another one. And soon there would be yet another trial; Lieutenant Colonel Marquez would raise his head but still look as though he were checking his fingernails, and he would ask Bob to ask the interpreter to raise his right hand and swear to translate according to the truth . . .

"Do you swear . . ."

"I do . . ."

Raising my right hand.

Neither then nor before had they asked me who I was. The oath I took could have been administered to anyone. The oath of an official interpreter.

———————

There was always a new case. One was that of a woman on her way into the village, pushing her baby buggy, and suddenly finding herself surrounded by some very friendly black soldiers, who started by laughing and joking with her but who gradually grew bolder and tried to kiss her. Frightened, she tried to flee. They caught her. There she was, torn from the buggy, dragged into the bushes—the buggy pushed into the ditch. It's no use screaming, no one can hear her, the village is far away. Now she's on her back. They try to force her. She fights and manages to escape. She runs. One of her attackers grabs his carbine and shoots.

Another concerned a poor farmer, around thirty years old, who went over to his neighbor's to help thresh the wheat. During the afternoon, he receives word that his wife is calling for help. He runs home and finds his wife thrown across the big bed, one black man lying on top of her, another holding her feet. A third man is sitting down, holding the hand of her two-year-old daughter. A fourth is guarding the door. This guard is shoved aside by the young farmer, who pulls his wife away from her assaulters. He pushes her out the door, she flees in one direction, he in the other, but the guard fires and the woman falls.

She dies that evening in the hospital.

"Ask the witness . . . How old was his wife?"

"Twenty-eight."

"And for how long had he been married?"

"Three years . . ."

"And does he recognize these men?"

He recognized all of them. "It was that one who fired . . ." He raised his right hand again as if to show he'd swear to it.

"Ask the witness to say, in his own words . . ."

And as soon as it was over and the verdict had been pronounced:

"Be kind enough to take the witness to the treasury officer."

The witness was given his witness pay, which came to two vacation days—a few hundred francs.

When we got out of there, I asked him, "Is that all?"

"Yes."

"A few hundred francs?"

Well, yes. He didn't see why I was asking him.

"But what are you going to do now?"

He had no idea. All alone, with his sorrow and his little girl to raise.

"They didn't talk to you about anything else?"

"No."

"And you didn't ask for anything, did you?"

What should he have asked for? He had no idea.

"What! Your wife is killed, and you're going off like this with a few hundred francs? The least they could do would be to give you money to help you raise your little girl! Get a lawyer and ask him what can be done in a case like this. If you want, I'll go with you."

"You're right," he answered, "I'll talk to our priest."

An officer passing by—he was one of the members of the military court—stopped and looked at us. He walked over and asked me if everything was all right. Did the witness have anything else to say?

"It's just that after getting his witness pay he was wondering . . ."

"Oh, I see! But you shouldn't be giving any advice."

I told the officer that it was too late and I already had.

He left. A little later I realized I should have talked to Bob about this issue and that in any case I was probably wrong to worry about it. Could anyone believe that the army and the government of a great democracy like the United States would do nothing more for the civilian victims for which their men were responsible than send them home with nothing to show for it but a few hundred francs from their witness indemnity? Plus a few cartons of cigarettes? No one could believe that, and I had only myself to blame for my negative thoughts.

But why didn't they tell me anything? Why had they never said anything? And why did this officer come along and inform me in that tone of his that I wasn't supposed to give any advice?

Since the start of the campaign for President Roosevelt's successor, Bob has been practically incapable of paying the slightest attention to anything else, unless, of course, an investigation is going on. Other than that, he seems indifferent to everything. As soon as he has a free moment, he walks through the school, stopping here and there to chat with one guy or another, commenting on the posters glued to the panels—posters spread throughout headquarters—and when we go out on an investigation, he starts talking again with Lieutenant Bradford about the presidential elections.

In the evening, I sit on the grass under the big oak tree in front of the school gates. There's always the same little crowd of young folk.

The other night Stef Markov showed up, and both that night and the next, the insolent freckled kid who waits on us at the mess hall, a young thug from New York, according to Bob. A very appealing young thug. Stef Markov was dressed to the nines, very smart, brushed, all his leather shining. We greeted each other; in other words, we exchanged winks.

"Nice weather, huh? Really nice evening."

We heard accordion music nearby. Everyone hurried over to watch. I went with the others and I saw that some young people had organized a dance in a barn. About a hundred young men and women were dancing under the lanterns. At the back of the barn were tables; you could sit and have a beer.

I sat down at one of the tables and stayed there, watching. I ordered a beer and lit my pipe. Bill came over. He sat next to me. I offered him a beer but he preferred lemonade. He had been taking a little walk before going back up to his room, but he had heard the accordion as he was leaving the base. That's what attracted him.

He found the spectacle very gay, quite a surprise. That

made him happy. A moment of relaxation, right? A dance! This would be a fresh note in his war diary. You can't always think about serious things, can you now? You can certainly have some wholesome fun. In the crowd, I noticed the young thug from New York dancing with a tall, beautiful girl. He went at it wholeheartedly. We left rather late.

———————

The next morning as I was crossing the courtyard at headquarters, a pudgy, moon-faced little man wearing gold-rimmed glasses approached me—he was an officer.

He strode hurriedly toward me and asked me if I was really the interpreter. I said yes. To which he answered that he was the rabbi and that he'd be very happy if I would be willing to go out on a mission. It was to look for the Jews who might still be in town and bring them to headquarters.

Of course I agreed. I would go to the city hall right away for the information. He accompanied me to the door of the base, walking slowly now and chatting. He wanted to know if I was a Gaullist. And what I thought of the political situation in France. And why we had so many political parties. He'd been told there were forty-eight of them in France. Didn't I think that was ridiculous? The Americans only had two. That's why everything worked so well there.

When we got to the gates, we met up with Lieutenant Colonel Marquez. Since the military court didn't meet that day, he was taking a constitutional. I left him with the rabbi.

———————

It was a beautiful day. The city was quite lively, it was market day. At the city hall they gave me a name, an address, directions. Ten minutes later I came to an old gray house with small windows shut tight and a narrow, unpainted door that I had only to push open.

At the end of a dark corridor I found a wooden staircase. Beneath my military boots the stairway resonated like a drum. I encountered no one. On the top floor (the fourth) I only found one door. I knocked but no one answered. I knocked a little harder and waited. Still no answer.

I was about to leave when the door opened slowly and the wrinkled face of an old woman, disheveled, aged seventy-five or more, stared at me in fear. A toothless mouth, wispy hair, an intense gaze . . .

I told her the rabbi had sent me; the rabbi wished that she and all those of her faith who might be in town would come to the school where the American troops were staying.

She opened the door. I entered a nearly empty room. Without saying a word, the old woman went straight to a dresser and opened a drawer. She took out some photos and spread them on a table: pictures of her children and her nephews whom the Germans had come and taken away. Once they took three of them at the same time. She told me without tears, then put the photos back in the drawer and showed me into the next room, where a bald old man with sunken cheeks, sunken eyes, and a long white beard was lying on a cot—a dying Job . . .

When he learned that I was sent by the rabbi, he held out a cold, skeletal hand and found the strength to ask me to thank the rabbi and tell him to please forgive him for not responding to his invitation since he was too weak.

I took my leave of the old Job, and we went back into the first room. There the old woman told me that she herself would accept the rabbi's invitation and that she'd make it her business to tell the others. It wouldn't take long—there weren't more than five of them.

She opened the door and we looked at one another, we didn't know what to say. Finally, I asked her why she hadn't answered right away when I knocked. But I understood from looking at her that I shouldn't have asked her that question. How could I not understand the terror that had gripped her when she heard the sound of my boots on the stairs?

———

I walked downstairs slowly, forcing myself to make the least possible noise. I found the street full of sun and people, and I wandered around for quite a while without a thought in my head, vaguely staring at the shop windows. I had wanted to find one or two bottles of perfume for Bob. It would have made him so happy!

All the Americans were crazy about the idea of bringing French perfume back to their wives. I went into two beauty salons but didn't find any there. They told me the Germans had made off with it all a long time ago.

Seeing me arrive in my handsome military garb, people thought I was an American, they spoke to me in jibberish or in their high school English, and when I told them that I was French they seemed to think I had played a joke on them. They grew suspicious, wanted to know where I came from and what I was doing there. Interpreter? Aha! And are they friendly, the Americans? Yes, very friendly. Why wouldn't they be? And are they going to stay around here for long? Who's to say? Until the Germans holed up in Brest surrender . . .

I kept strolling through the streets, and in the fourth or fifth shop I finally found exactly what I was looking for. Two bottles of perfume. I stuffed them in my pocket, went back to the base, and looked for Bob, but Bob wasn't there.

———

In my comings and goings at headquarters, I heard about a very ugly incident that had just taken place in a village inside the combat zone. The murder of a Free French fighter by a Ranger officer.

It had happed late the night before while we were at the dance. As the Resistance fighter was leaving the café where he had spent the evening drinking with an American officer, the officer had followed him and from three steps behind had fired the entire contents of his gun into his back.

I went to the garage. Joe wasn't there. I didn't see the jeep. The day came to an end, the officers didn't appear at the mess hall. After leaving the mess I returned to the garage, the jeep still wasn't there. So I thought I'd go sit for a while under the big oak tree, but as I approached the gate, I saw that there was no one under the oak. On such a beautiful evening!

The sentry was alone at the gate. I wanted to know what was going on, and I asked the sentry; he responded with a growl. He was in a very bad mood. He didn't give a damn what was going on! And just as well he was on duty, because if it weren't for that . . . No way! He hoped not. Those bastards! He wouldn't have gone anyway, because, you know . . .

He was looking at me strangely, smiling sadly. He started counting on the five fingers of his right hand. I had no idea what he was acting out. Sticking out the thumb of his left finger, he placed it on the tip of each finger of his right hand, as if he were picking out notes on a piano, and while he did this, still smiling the same way, he murmured something I didn't understand. Ah! He was spelling a word. Could that be it?

"The Bible?"

"Yes, of course. B-I-B-L-E."

What did the Bible have to do with anything? And what luck he was on duty, because if it weren't for that . . . he said. And without the Bible, of course! No way! At least he hoped not! But what a bunch of bastards! Real pigs, all of them! That's why there was no one here at the gates and not many people at the base either. Just look at the courtyards, no one was around.

"So . . . where are they?"

"Why don't you take a walk in town and see," he answered with a forced laugh.

That's what I did. I didn't need to go far. In a narrow little street I saw a long line of GIs along the sidewalk, stretching all the way down the street——more than a hundred of them. It was the opening of a bordello.

———————

. . . I didn't stay there. I went back to headquarters, and as I was entering, the sentry said, "Well? Did you see it?"

"Yes."

"Pigs!"

I didn't answer. I walked a few steps into the courtyard, but the sentry called me back to tell me that Lieutenant Stone had just come in and was looking for me. I should go see Joe in the garage. They might still be together.

"Something strange seems to be going on. Someone killed a guy around here, in a restaurant."

"Is that so? What about it?"

I caught sight of the jeep; Joe was still behind the wheel. Bob jumped out of the car while Joe stopped the motor. I didn't see Lieutenant Bradford. Bob came running to greet me; he led me right toward the kitchens, walking very fast— he started out by telling me he'd had quite enough of this filthy business, he was wiped out, exhausted, fed up, and now, with this shit hole of a case to deal with!

"One nasty story, you can believe me."

I probably already knew all about it. Everyone around here was probably talking about it. That son of a bitch! All his ammunition in the guy's back.

"I've had it up to here. I'm not cut out for this. I'm a lawyer. It's the army that's turned me into a prosecutor. If you think I'm enjoying this, God almighty! The bastard! He'd just returned from the front lines when he went into the hotel bar;

the other guy was already there. They started drinking together. And according to the only witness we've been able to talk to until now—you know, don't be surprised if I didn't ask you to come out on the investigation with us, because one of our agents showed up early this morning, an intelligence officer——he acted as interpreter, he was the one who questioned the waitress. Well, according to the waitress the two men seemed very pleased with each other at first. But wait. Let's find a corner where we can sit down."

We went into the kitchen and sat down at the first table. I expected to see the young thug from New York, but he wasn't there. Instead, there was a tall guy, a bit overweight, very tanned; Bob ordered tea from him and whatever there was to eat. Before continuing his story, he told me to take a good look at the guy who was serving us: an Indian, a real, full-blooded redskin.

And then, devouring his food, he went on to tell me how—still according to the waitress—the two men started arguing a little, around ten or eleven at night. They had each already had quite a lot to drink. The waitress couldn't say what might have been the reason for their argument, but she thought she had figured out that the American officer was demanding something that the other man was refusing to do. She thought it was something the Frenchman had in his pocket and didn't want to show.

They had raised their voices, and the waitress got scared, thinking they'd end up in a fight. But instead they calmed down and started drinking again, sitting at the bar until midnight. Then the Frenchman left through a door in back that let out onto a courtyard. The other guy followed him and fired at his back, using all the ammunition in his gun. Dirty son of a bitch!

"All right. Let's go to bed. There's nothing like a good night's sleep."

The next morning, after the mess hall, Lieutenant Bradford led me into a room where I saw the waitress from the hotel, witness number one, a girl of less than twenty, sitting on the edge of a table. She was swinging her legs. A young country girl dressed in her finest, rosy-faced and blond, bright eyed, a pretty girl who had gotten herself dolled up as if she were going to a party and who giggled whenever she spoke. There were two officers with her.

One of them was questioning the girl. The other, leaning over a table, was studying a map. I realized that the two officers were the intelligence agents.

The moment I heard the officer who was interrogating the waitress speak, I realized that his French was perfect, with no mistakes and no accent. We'd hardly been there a minute when a young lieutenant arrived, as much of a stranger to me as the two officers, accompanied by a twelve-year-old boy. Lieutenant Bradford introduced me to his young colleague: Lieutenant Reginald Bryant—they called him Reggie. The plan was for him to take over Bob's job. The little boy was the son of a French family, friends of Lieutenant Bradford.

Since the boy wasn't feeling well, Lieutenant Bradford had decided to take him to a doctor he knew in a hospital in the country. They were going right away. Before leaving the room I just had time to hear the officer ask the young waitress if she could say what the argument had been about.

Yes, she thought she could say that the American officer asked the Frenchman to show him his papers. The Frenchman refused. She was all the more convinced it was that because she remembered later that the Frenchman had said to her: "Can you imagine? He wants me to show him my papers! No kidding! American or not, I don't have to show him my papers, not me; I never showed them to the Boches!"

Lieutenant Bradford had already opened the door, and Reggie was leading the little boy out. I was the last to go.

The second intelligence officer was still leaning over his map. He was tracing something with his pencil. The young girl kept swinging her legs. I joined Lieutenant Bradford, Reggie, and the child. Joe was standing next to the jeep, smoking a cigarette. When he saw us coming, he took his place behind the wheel. We got into the car, Lieutenant Bradford next to Joe, young Lieutenant Reggie and I in back with the little boy between us.

"OK, Joe."

The poor little boy! He was pale as a ghost and totally silent.

On the way, I learned that the doctor we were going to see—the head doctor in a hospital in the country—had known the defendant, and that he would be an important character witness. The trial was to take place any day now. Reggie would act as prosecutor and Bob as defense lawyer. That was why Bob hadn't come along with us. He had to meet with the waitress from the hotel and with the intelligence officers. Reggie would be the one to take the doctor's testimony.

The little boy still wasn't talking, he still looked just as unhappy.

"Please tell him not to be afraid," Reggie asked me. "We aren't going to hurt him."

I asked Reggie what the child was suffering from. He answered that he really didn't know what it was, except for a kind of listlessness. During the occupation he hadn't been able to eat his fill. They were going to examine him thoroughly, do some tests, take x-rays, probably keep him in the hospital for a day or two.

I explained all that to the boy. He smiled at me. And we pursued our way that morning across the grayish countryside.

Reggie reminded me of Bill, even though he wasn't a giant like him—far from it!—and he was two or three years older.

Just like Bill, Reggie was a really good, honest kid, very wholesome. A fine, innocent young man.

After many detours across the back roads, we came to a large meadow, long, flat, all green, surrounded by trees. It was here, far from the world, that the hospital had been set up: long, gray canvas tents, brand-new. It was starting to drizzle. After getting out of the car, Lieutenant Bradford observed that we were exactly on time. He complimented Joe, telling him he was as punctual as the railroad. Joe accepted the compliment with a smile and a wink.

Joe stayed in the jeep; we entered one of the tents. The head doctor was expecting us. He too began by congratulating us on our promptness, with the tone of voice, gestures, and smile of a gentleman——soft spoken, thoughtful, knowing, conscious of his superiority perhaps, but not forgetting for a moment what he owed others. A rather tall, slender man with white hair.

"Ah, here is our little patient . . . Very good! We are going to take care of him," he said, tenderly patting the boy's head. Then, speaking to me: "You're the interpreter, I presume? Very glad to meet you. Tell this young man that we are going to take care of him and that we won't hurt him! Tell him. We'll probably keep him for a day or two, and you'll come for him, won't you, Lieutenant Bradford? Tell him we have such nice nurses here that he won't want to leave! Hmmm. He doesn't look well."

All the little things he said as he led us into his office were merely words of kindness for everyone, a form of courtesy, a friendly welcome. In each of his words, in the least of his gestures, his glances, there appeared to be real warmth, but you also felt he was very much in control and must know just how to manage his time.

He kept his hand on the boy's neck and guided him gently forward toward his office, where he asked us all to sit down. He let go of the child and remained standing for a minute, just long enough to tell us that when he occasionally had time to take a stroll, back where he lived, he really liked to see children in the streets. There were always a lot of children at play, looking in shop windows or out on some errand like everyone else, and as he passed by, he liked to pat a child's head. To feel a child's head under his hand.

"Most of the time they don't even notice . . . But once in a while you'll find one who turns around and smiles at you. Good. And now," he concluded as he sat down, "let's talk about serious matters."

Lieutenant Bradford seemed rather embarrassed. Were we going to deal with the little boy first . . . or were we . . .

"No, Doctor, we have to talk about . . . you know, that unfortunate incident . . ."

"Oh!" the head doctor exclaimed. "Of course," he said, as he pushed a button.

Another doctor arrived and the head doctor had him take the child away. They asked me to accompany them, and we went into a consulting room. The two lieutenants and the head doctor stayed together.

With what care, what solicitude, what precautions the doctors and nurses tended the boy! With what artful tenderness, humor, consideration, and firmness! The boy was questioned, examined, turned around and around, every which way, so that he actually thought it was a game. Around him, nothing but smiling faces, measured gestures, never any haste, an atmosphere of security, so much so that by the end, when I was asked to tell him that they were going to keep him for two or three days, after which Lieutenant Reggie would come for him, he responded with a happy smile.

They put him in a wheelchair, more to amuse him than out of necessity. He let them do it. Such was the serene image I had when I left the little patient to return to the head doctor's office. They were done, and were waiting for me to get back so they could leave.

After asking me for news of the little patient and hearing that they were going to keep him for two or three days, the head doctor said, "OK," and moved toward the door.

The time he had planned to devote to us had expired. Nothing remained but what good manners dictated, and so, in the calmest fashion, as if he had nothing else to do, he accompanied us to the jeep with a totally relaxed stride. As he walked, he summed up what he had just said to the lieutenants:

"I'll tell you again, and I regret having to tell you: he is a killer!" Several times he repeated, "He is a killer . . ."

The two lieutenants walked beside him, looking down.

"He is a killer!" the head doctor repeated yet again. "I know him well, alas!"

Hadn't this killer only recently gunned down as many men as there were bullets in his gun from a row of prisoners?

He'd said afterwards that he didn't like the way the men were looking at him.

"Well that's the gist of what I can tell you about him, and believe me, I'm sorry to have to do it."

When we left the hospital, young Lieutenant Reggie seemed completely different. Lieutenant Bradford, too. Both of them were very quiet, Lieutenant Bradford even quieter than usual, but he was too well bred to change his normal behavior—he had too much self-respect and respect for others to stoop to confidences. But all that was on both of their minds was the way the head doctor had kept insisting, "He is a killer." If a man like him could affirm such a thing, he was to be taken at his word. You could be sure he had considered the weight of his testimony.

We were driving slowly. There was no reason to hurry back, Lieutenant Bradford said. We might even take time to stop and have a bite to eat somewhere. There were always rations in the jeep.

Joe seemed perplexed; for once he didn't know which route to take.

We were very close to Brest, which we'd been hearing rumors about. Several times we had noticed small groups of Free Frenchmen in the fields, crouching in the hollows made by grenades. It was still drizzling. We were crossing large empty stretches of barren countryside, dotted with little black rocks, and once, in the distance, on a barren mound, we spotted a chapel. Lieutenant Bradford didn't mention stopping anymore. Joe kept going. Wherever he was taking us now, we were sure that as soon as he got his orders he'd find the right road and get us back to headquarters.

Suddenly someone said: "And do you know what the other guy was doing?"

It was Lieutenant Bradford who had asked the question. The other guy? Who could he mean? The other intelligence officer, the one who was studying the map.

He had been studying the itinerary of the "spy" since landing in France. According to the papers found on the victim's body . . .

"Are you going to make him out to be a spy?"

"Why do you say that, Louis? Intelligence is going to say he is . . ."

He didn't say anything else. Neither did I. Reggie hadn't spoken. As for Joe, given his position as a mere driver, he probably thought he never had the right to say anything, even though he was a citizen of the greatest democracy in the world.

We wandered around for a while longer, sometimes in the midst of troops, sometimes through areas that were deserted. We drove through villages swarming with soldiers. Lieutenant Bradford gave the order to head back. Joe found the main road and Reggie remembered the rations.

We found them and started to munch on some crackers.

Suddenly Lieutenant Bradford ordered Joe to stop and cut off the motor.

"Listen!" he said.

We perked up our ears: silence, the deepest silence.

"My God," the lieutenant exclaimed. "It's over!"

We were deep in the countryside. Around us as far as the eye could see was nothing but land, fields, woods, rolling hills, barely a distant steeple in the gray drizzle, and not a sound except for the familiar sounds of the earth, not a shell exploding, not a machine gun firing, nothing: the whinnying of a horse.

It was true. The Germans had just surrendered.

If we had had any doubts about it, we quickly had proof when a convoy of prisoners passed us, their jackets unbuttoned and their hands clasped behind their necks, standing packed together on open trucks.

The convoy was moving slowly. Since they had nothing to hang onto, the prisoners were swaying from side to side like rag dolls. Men with blank looks. We stayed at the side of the road, waiting until we could move again. But the convoy was followed by another—a medical convoy—which was joined by a third: returning American troops.

Joe himself didn't dream of starting up amid that mob. No sooner had the medical convoy passed when yet another convoy of prisoners arrived, as long as the first one and just like it, with men standing on the open trucks, their jackets open and their hands clasped behind their heads. Lieutenant Bradford suddenly looked at me intently.

"I can tell what you're thinking."

"Yes," I answered. "Aren't you?"

He shrugged his shoulders, a sign of helplessness, perhaps of resignation, certainly disgust. "I didn't like the way they were looking at me," the Ranger officer had said after firing on as many prisoners as there was ammunition in his gun. Of course that's what I was thinking; he was, too.

The last truck passed; Joe made up his mind, he shifted into gear, and we took to the road again.

It wasn't easy getting back. The news was spreading everywhere, the roads were blocked with cars and trucks, the villages were swarming with troops, there were thousands of prisoners to evacuate, wounded men, refugees. We heard that Brest was three-fourths destroyed, nothing was left of the ports, the arsenal, the docks, the piers . . .

When we reached headquarters, three huge trucks that had just arrived—the drivers were still at the wheel—were parked in the middle of the courtyard, and men were swarming around them, trying to grab something and leave as quickly as possible. They were trucks captured from the Germans and brought straight here, packed with bottles of liquor, cognac, rum, Cointreau, vodka. The men came, helped themselves, and took off quickly without paying any attention to the drivers, who were shouting themselves hoarse that this part of the spoils was strictly for officers!

"Strictly for officers, you jerks, you sons of bitches! You're going to get screwed. The military court's right over there!"

Lieutenant Bradford's arrival sent the looters scrambling. The lieutenants decided they wouldn't make a big deal over a few bottles of liquor. As long as they didn't do it again. After all, it was a day of victory.

The first thing Bill did when he saw me coming was to show me his war diary. In large writing, underscored with two thick black lines, he had just noted the date, September 18, below which I read: "The surrender of the Germans trapped in Brest took place today, September 18, at three in the afternoon. After forty-three days of siege and four years and three months of occupation." This was written in very large letters and underlined. Next, Bill had left a blank space, then, in regular handwriting, he had noted: "Yesterday we heard that several small German towns had fallen to the Allies. Nancy was liberated by French troops. The Germans are retreating everywhere. VICTORY!" The word "victory," like the date, was in capitals, underlined twice.

He told me he didn't think he had the right to keep a war diary, but since in his diary he only gave personal impressions or recorded major dates like today's, and of course never revealed military secrets, he thought he could go on keeping it, for he was absolutely certain that if it ever fell into enemy hands, the enemy couldn't do anything with it.

"And of course they won't!"

"Good for you, Bill! Do you have any news of Lieutenant Stone?"

"Bob?"

"Yes, Bob."

"Bob? I saw him this afternoon walking with one of his friends. So you're still dealing with your blacks? More of their dirty goings-on with women?"

"No, Bill. Not right now."

Was it possible he hadn't heard about the "nasty incident"? Indeed, he had. He had heard about it, but only vaguely. A murder, right? With a Ranger officer involved?

"That's right, Bill. And Reggie, Lieutenant Reggie—do you know him?"

"Oh, Reggie! Of course. A very sensitive young man."

"We took a child to a hospital in the country, a twelve-year-old from a family who are friends of Reggie's."

"Oh that's good. Very good. We really love children back home."

"I know, Bill."

"And we still don't love them enough, because if we loved them better we'd be a little more energetic about changing the world."

He closed his war diary. I told him about the prisoner convoys on the roads, men standing in open trucks with their jackets open and their hands clasped behind their necks, swaying from side to side.

"You should have seen it, Bill!"

"I'll see it soon at our army movies. Our newsreels are really well done. And you know that our prisoners are very well treated. We're democrats and we wage war without hatred. Haven't you heard it said that, for us, war is not an exercise in passions, it's a laboratory . . . ?"

———

The end of that day of victory was like all the others. We neither drank nor sang. At the mess hall I saw the people feeding themselves as on any other day with their excellent canned goods, corn, and pastries made with honey, and drinking tea or hot chocolate or Nescafé according to their taste. The tenor of the conversations was, as usual, that of an assembly of decent fellows who, since childhood, had learned how to "control themselves."

When I left the mess hall it was still too early to go to bed. It had stopped drizzling a while ago. The only reasonable thing to do at the end of the evening was to sit under the oak tree.

As I was heading there, someone stopped me and asked if I'd like to go with him to a nearby house, where something strange was going on. I followed him. As we went, I saw there were already some people under the big oak. Because the grass was wet, people had brought benches and chairs. Bob was there, chatting with someone I didn't know, probably the friend Bill had told me about.

Still following my guide, we got to a small, middle-class house that looked abandoned. On the ground floor, in a large room with no furniture except for a table, were a few infantrymen and three women. On the ground and along the walls—weapons. Ammunition belts on the floor, rifles leaning against the walls. In the middle of this arsenal, three girls, all quite young, were walking around, laughing loudly, now looking at the men teasingly, now pretending to ignore their presence, now adjusting their hose, now dabbing on lipstick or powdering their faces.

The men were biting their thumbs. I heard one of them mutter that he really didn't want to get the clap. They wanted to know who the girls were, where they came from. But wherever they came from, all three were probably whores who had worked in a German whorehouse, lost in the debacle— which didn't keep them from skipping around, didn't prevent them from tapping their high heels on the floor like horses, didn't make them laugh any less idiotically as they cast lustful glances at one soldier or another, turning, twirling in their cheap, flashy clothes——pink, mauve, green . . . Maybe they were drunk?

I warned the men who they were and suggested they be careful. One of them, very angry, answered, God knows why, that "all this" was the Jews' fault, since they were every-where . . .

"A Goldstein here . . . an Epstein there . . ."

————————

As I was nearing the big oak tree, Reggie stood up and greeted me. He took me aside:

"Do you know who he's with?"

I didn't need to ask him who he was talking about. He meant Lieutenant Stone. He was there under the oak tree with his friend.

"He's with the defendant's brother," Reggie told me.

"Oh?"

"Apparently they spent the whole day together."

I told Reggie it was only natural that a brother . . .

"Maybe so," he answered sadly. "You know that the trial's set for tomorrow morning? And that Lieutenant Stone will be the defense lawyer? And that you won't be asked to partici-pate?"

That didn't surprise me. Besides, it was quite normal. The presence of the two intelligence officers made my participation perfectly useless.

————————

The trial started at nine o'clock. Just as Reggie had told me, I wasn't summoned. I took a walk. I caught sight of the rabbi with a number of people around him: the last few Jews brought together by the poor old woman.

At noon, the trial was over: acquittal . . .

. . . He entered the mess hall accompanied by Lieutenant Colonel Marquez and a few members of the court who acted as a kind of escort. Bob appeared a bit later, but it was the other one I saw first: an ogre. Just as in fairy tales. The killer. A big fat ogre with a large red face, grinning from ear to ear.

Two days later, we left in a convoy for an unknown destination. But there was no doubt that we were headed north, probably toward Belgium. I didn't know my neighbors in the truck I was sitting in.

Where Lieutenants Stone and Bradford, Reggie, and Joe had gone, I didn't know. And Bill? I was sitting in the front of a truck, we were driving on the left; on the right were huge trucks and pieces of artillery. We drove through cities and small towns. The people cheered us on, raising their hands and making the V sign with their fingers.

We drove all morning. It wasn't until around one in the afternoon that the convoy stopped on the side of the road. All the men got out. Rations were handed out; the men sat down as comfortably as they could on the embankment. Our break didn't even last ten minutes.

At nightfall we went through the town of Fougères, more than half of it in ruins, and our convoy stopped alongside a large meadow. We left the vehicles on the side of the road, and the men set up tents for the night at the highest part of the meadow.

Down below, behind a hedge, ran a stream. The sun was setting. An old farmer appeared from behind the hedge, on his way back from fishing. He smiled at us and said good evening. When the men saw the old farmer, they thought he might be able to find them something fresh to eat. I asked him if this was possible. He said they could always take a look around. Four of us went, the old farmer, two of the soldiers, and me.

The old man led us to some farms. We were welcomed everywhere. People gave us butter, eggs. They didn't want any money. No matter how hard I insisted that we wanted to pay and that we could, they never agreed.

We returned to the camp with our provisions, but when the officers saw what they were, they declared that the men could eat the eggs or make omelets if they liked, but they forbade them to touch the butter, which wasn't pasteurized.

Then a lady arrived and just from the sound of her voice it was clear that she was a wealthy farmer's wife. A tall, beautiful woman, heavyset, in her forties. She was coming to invite the officers to dinner at her house.

The officers responded with great courtesy. Unfortunately it wasn't possible for them to accept her invitation. That was something not permitted to officers on active duty. The good lady left again, a little disappointed but fully understanding, having asked the officers what she might do to assist them or simply what might please them. They replied that they needed nothing and they thanked her very warmly.

The old farmer was still there. He was watching with great interest the men who were putting up the tents, a task they had almost finished. He thought they were doing a good job and working fast.

"And you," he asked me, "wouldn't you like to come for a bowl of soup at our house? Everyone would be pleased."

I answered that I'd like to but would have to ask the colonel's permission. Which I did. The colonel said I was welcome to go, but only if I could figure out before I left which tent I was going to sleep in so I wouldn't wake anyone when

I came back, and also that I must not forget the password, which he would give me. We were out in the field now, and we needed to take things very seriously.

At the dinner table, the mother starts telling the story after her husband has said, "Tell him, Maman Flore. Tell him what happened in the château." All those gathered around the table, her husband, her daughters, Jérôme her oldest son, are prepared to listen attentively and respectfully even though each of them could have told the same story.

It was a few weeks earlier, in a place called Croix-Saint-Bernard in Commander Brémont's château. To make things perfectly clear, she first explained that that château was a good ten miles from here, two miles from the nearest village, that it was an estate of several dozen acres: meadows, woods, fields.

Since returning from the war in 1918, Commander Brémont had lived alone with Céline, his servant. The château was a beautiful, hundred-year-old residence.

When he returned from the war, Commander Brémont was forty. Maman Flore described him as a very handsome man, the last descendant of an old family, living in the old ways, doing little other than taking care of his lands and hunting, hardly ever receiving visitors, reading a great deal. Céline was a local girl.

"Poor Céline! We were the same age, the two of us. She would have been fifty-five next November, as I'll be in December. We went to school together, we took our catechism together and our First Communion. Her parents were servants, like mine. Only I got married, she didn't. There was nothing she would have liked better, but the one she wanted was killed in the war, in 1916. Her two brothers as well. So she went to town to work as a maid for a while but she didn't like it. She came back here. Her parents were dead. She worked here and there on farms until the day she went to work for Monsieur Brémont. That must have been around 1924, 1925. Life had become more or less peaceful again. Céline and I must have been thirty-five . . ."

According to Maman Flore, Céline, at twenty, had been a very pretty, sturdy girl, a beautiful flower, a tall, healthy country girl, well endowed, with strong hands, big bones, brown skin. When she returned from town, she had hardened, especially in her face. As she reached thirty, a beautiful woman in full bloom, she exuded a sense of strength, an almost animal-like solidity. She hardly ever laughed. Something hard had set in behind her rather narrow forehead, and she had taken to pressing her lips together whether she was answering yes or no, in a way that made her look bitter. And yes and no were about the only words she uttered all day long.

"As far as what they were to each other, that was nobody's business."

Having said that, Maman Flore remained silent for a long time, her hands crossed on the table, gazing into the distance.

At that point her oldest son, Jérôme, carefully pulled his wallet from his pocket and took something out, which he slid toward me without saying a word: a photo of Céline. A fairly recent photo. Seeing me pick up the photo, the mother came out of her reverie.

"Yes, there she is. You see I haven't lied to you!"

Indeed she hadn't! It was exactly the face I had imagined as I was listening to her, the face of a fifty-year-old country woman that time and the seasons had done their work on, like the face on an old Calvary cross.* A solid head, the hair pulled back under a small white linen bonnet, a hard bony face, still very handsome, truly the face of a woman in full vigor, knowing what she wanted and wanting it more than anyone. You could see it in her chin, from the severity of her mouth, from her forehead; it was clear she had never hung her head.

"That's her," Maman Flore started in again, "and as you see, she doesn't look very easygoing! But in spite of that, you mustn't think she was a bad person, far from it! She never wronged anyone or let any problem come near her without sorting it out. Only she didn't talk. But she did what needed to be done. And Commander Brémont wasn't a big talker either. He didn't avoid people, but he didn't seek them out either. He could stop on the road and exchange a few words with someone he met, give advice if you asked him, and it seems his advice was always well worth taking. Day after day, he always took care of his domain, his tenant farms, his wood cutting; went hunting when the season came; spent hours reading by his fire in winter or on his terrace in summer."

Even in the village they rarely saw him. People often wondered why the commander hadn't gone into politics. He would have made a good mayor. But for years the commander hadn't wanted anything to do with things like that.

So the years passed by, and the Second World War started. The Germans invaded the country. Despite his age——he had just turned sixty——the commander enlisted again. Before the invasion he'd been seen in uniform, then had disappeared for quite a while; by the time he returned home, the Germans were already all over the country.

---

*A Calvary cross, or *calvaire*, is the central piece of statuary in many villages in Brittany. Set on a granite base, it is a stone cross representing the Crucifixion, often decorated with figures of local saints or scenes from Christ's Passion.

Céline hadn't left the château. He started to live with her again as he'd always done before, dividing his time between the management of his estate, his wood cutting, his tenant farms, on which life had become so difficult; he had started doing some work himself, going from farm to farm, helping and encouraging everyone. Older than sixty, he was still the same handsome man, robust and capable of working as hard and as long as any farmer.

It was the end of that first year of the occupation. The Germans were everywhere in the towns and in the villages. Sometimes you could see a detail passing on the roads, but they never came to the château.

It was in the following year that Maman Flore had first heard about what was going on at the château. Now you could talk about it because the Liberation was here. What she had heard then was about the escaped prisoners they hid in the château long enough to find them a way to live out in the open with false papers, about furtive visits to the commander by foreigners, and, soon after——the next year——people were talking about weapons hidden on the land, aviators gathering at the château and then leaving for the coast, where they were picked up by a British gunboat.

In 1943, when obligatory work service in Germany was decreed, the commander opened his doors to many young people who refused to leave for Germany. That was how the Croix-Saint-Bernard underground or *maquis* was formed, with Commander Brémont in charge. From then on its members lived in the château and in the woods, training daily for war, practicing surprise attacks, burning German cars, derailing trains, and blowing up pylons. Their group was reinforced by volunteers from town; among these were two brothers, one between eighteen and twenty, the other around sixteen.

The Germans, it seemed, kept on ignoring the existence of this *maquis*, and things stayed that way until early spring, when the commander was secretly informed that the château was going to be attacked any day now, not by the Germans but by Darnand's militiamen.* A unit of two hundred. The commander immediately gave the order to disperse.

"We're not going to fight Frenchmen. Those people are nothing but traitors, and bandits besides, but they are French, and the Germans are here. We're not going to fight Frenchmen in full view of the enemy."

"That's exactly what he said, isn't it, Jérôme?" Maman Flore asked, turning to her son.

Yes, that was it, all right. The young men in the *maquis* had tried to convince the commander that they could resist. There were enough of them to do it. The commander stuck by his order. The Allies were about to land. He wasn't going to let his men get killed by those traitors when they would be desperately needed as soon as the Allies set foot on French soil. He, of course, would stay at the château and wait for the militiamen.

As for Céline, not for a second had she ever considered going into hiding. The men in the *maquis* had obeyed the commander's order, except for two of them—the two brothers from town.

Hidden behind a bush, Jérôme had seen Darnand's militiamen arrive: as expected, they were a detail of two hundred men under the command of a lieutenant. He had seen them enter through the main gate, cross the garden, and advance as a unit until they reached the château, which they surrounded. The lieutenant posted guards everywhere, then entered the château with some of his men . . .

*Darnand's *milice* was a French police squad formed by one of Pétain's right-hand men in 1943 to combat the strengthening armed resistance by the French. The *miliciens* (militiamen) were responsible for many acts of terror and murder during the last months of the Nazi occupation.

What happened next was told by the younger of the two brothers, who had managed to escape. The militia lieutenant called out to the commander, who was waiting at the top of the big staircase with Céline and the two young men at his side:

"What! You're not in uniform?" The commander did not respond to this sneering question. Nor to the one that fol-

lowed.

"Where are your men?"

No reply.

The militiamen started to invade the château and search everywhere. A dozen of them stayed with the lieutenant.

"Where are your weapons?"

A question to which neither Commander Brémont nor the two young men nor Céline responded.

"Aha! I see we're going to have to deal with this another way. They're all yours, boys!" the lieutenant exclaimed.

The "boys" in question leaped at the commander, at the young men, and at Céline and started beating them. That was when the younger of the two brothers managed to escape, he himself doesn't know how.

It was learned much later that the militiamen, after beating them as much as they could, had dragged off the commander and the older brother and had turned them over to the Germans. As for Céline, after torturing her for a long time, hoping to get the information they wanted from her, they realized they weren't going to succeed, and suffocated her between two mattresses. The château was looted from top to bottom. Jérôme, who had continued to watch them, following the orders he'd been given, had seen the militiamen leaving with two trucks full of loot. Jérôme had heard one them say to another— no doubt a young recruit they were trying to train: "Lucky for them there wasn't any resistance, because you know what we usually do in those cases? We burn! . . ."

It was very late when I left the farm. The father and Jérôme accompanied me all the way to camp. We walked without saying much to one another. When we got to the side of the road close to the camp, we stopped for a moment before parting, and the father took something out of his pocket and handed it to me, saying, "At least take this, you might be glad for a drop or two on the road!"

It was a little bottle of his own eau-de-vie. I tried to turn it down. He said he didn't see how I could dare to. Surely the Americans had some of everything, but eau-de-vie like that?

I took the bottle and stuffed it into my pocket. We shook hands and they left. I crossed the hedges at the edge of the field. In the bright moonlight I could see the tents all in a row and a guard, his gun on his shoulder, walking slowly between them.

We said good evening. The guard remarked how calm everything was and how warm the night was. At the end of the meadow, down by the stream, someone had built a fire. I walked toward it. A man was lying next to a small campfire. He said good evening. On such a warm night, he couldn't stand it inside a tent. After choosing a place to build his fire, he had gone to look for wood. And, by Jupiter, he was guilty of destroying a piece of fence to get a little dry wood, and he hoped God would forgive him for his sin.

"And what about you, are you going into a tent?"

I said no, and that with his permission I would stay next to the fire. "OK," he replied. And he closed his eyes.

I lay down in the grass by the fire, under the moon, still as beautiful, and the sky still as full of stars, and eventually I fell asleep—but not right away.

I still have to tell what happened next and how my journey came to an end. I had gotten as far as that night in the meadow by the campfire after my return from the supper where I'd heard Maman Flore tell her story. After an almost sleepless night—I had heard the guard's footsteps for hours—I finally dozed off, and when I woke up, it was broad daylight and they were already breaking camp. Less than an hour later we were on the road again. I saw we were heading for Paris.

In the jeep I was still surrounded by silent men I didn't know. Perhaps the men were a little more worried than the previous day. Even though the road was clear and you couldn't see a plane in the bright sky, no one forgot that the war wasn't over. Hadn't Hitler said many times that he would never surrender?

Like the day before, another convoy accompanied ours— a convoy of trucks carrying pieces of artillery, some of them enormous. As they passed by, they created a powerful gust of wind, which almost tipped over our lightweight jeeps. This was the army proper.

. . . The kind of indifference I'd been struggling with for months hadn't changed. And yet this was the event, and here I was at it, but as stranger. Perhaps I was feeling the effects of the terrible story our hostess had told the night before. A story which, alas, would be added to so many equally terrible stories of houses burned, young men hanged under balconies in village squares, roundups and massacres as in the darkest hours of ancient history.

We drove all day. We stopped only for a few moments along a country road—I have no idea where—to eat our rations. And then we drove on. It was always the same parade, the same trucks full of troops, the same pieces of artillery next to us.

When at one point my eyes fell on those cannons, I noticed that some of them had names written on them in large red letters, women's names—maybe the names of movie stars, but also . . . yes, I really saw it: "Death Dealer." And a little farther along, another one: "Widow-Maker."

―――――

So nothing had changed then, and probably never would.

"My boys, if you're going over there to keep the world the way it is, then stay home, but if you're going to change the world . . ." That poor bishop! And poor Bill, whom I'd probably run into tonight at the stopover, poor innocent child, as naive—alas—as I am.

We stopped for the night at Versailles. All I remember from that evening is the way one of the officers was incapable of speaking to you without asking, "How do you like my sweet Ohio accent?" He flew into a rage when he found out that the "the Krauts" had pillaged Versailles. For a good half hour he didn't stop insulting them, calling them sons of a bitch, dirty bastards, until finally, unable to go on, he retreated into his tent like everyone else . . .

I would have liked to see Lieutenant Stone and Bill again, but neither one appeared.

―――――

The night passed. The next day we drove through Paris, then took the road toward Compiègne, with the same beautiful sky, the same parade of huge cannons with their names in red letters.

————

Today we've been in Compiègne for nearly three days, a rather long stopover, during which I had the pleasant surprise of seeing Lieutenant Stone again. While we were parked in the middle of the town surrounded by a lot of people, someone came up to me, pushing the crowd aside, and planted himself in front of me.

"Hello, Louis, how are you? How do you like this little pleasure cruise? Nice weather, huh?"

It was Lieutenant Stone. Still the same Lieutenant Stone, healthy, good-natured, cheerful, his beautiful violinist's hand cordially reaching out for mine.

"Hello! How about yourself?"

"First-rate!" he answered.

"I hoped I'd see you yesterday at Versailles. Where were you?"

"Somewhere in France . . ." He added that he was happy, in any case, not to have to deal with those miserable courts-martial of black soldiers. They would certainly start up again one day, he didn't know where or how. But . . . whatever else might happen, this trip was a chance to relax. And what a beautiful country France was, wasn't it?

"Of course. Is our friend Bill still with you?"

"Naturally. Maybe you'll find him tonight in Saint-Quentin."

"We're going to Saint-Quentin?"

"Yes. But it's 'top secret.' You're not supposed to know anything about it."

"OK. How about Bill, is he still talking about his bishop all the time?"

"Yes, he is. And he's still keeping his war diary . . . to jog his memory," he added, and burst out laughing.

Lieutenant Stone's good humor was constant. But suddenly he seemed to darken. He looked at me almost severely.

"Say, old fellow, you don't look so good."

"Me?"

I didn't feel bad at all. Maybe a bit tired, but I'd been tired for so long that I paid no attention to it.

"We'll meet this evening in Saint-Quentin and talk about it."

"You think so?"

"Yes I do. Right now we're leaving again. We're getting back in the trucks in a minute. OK, Louis, see you tonight!"

"See you tonight."

"OK. Take care of yourself!"

"OK, thanks. See you tonight."

He disappeared, pushing the crowd aside as he had done when he arrived. A little farther on I saw him running . . .

———

As good as his word, Lieutenant Stone looked me up as soon as we arrived in Saint-Quentin. The first thing he told me when he reached me was that he was inviting me to have dinner with him and a few other officers, some of whom I knew since they had served in the military court, including Lieutenant Bradford, of course. We were to dine at the hotel.

"Is that OK with you?"

"Why not?"

"And how did the trip go?"

"Fine."

Lieutenant Stone told me he had made the trip in the company of an officer, a veteran of the First World War, who recognized, as we were approaching Saint-Quentin, the places where he had fought back then and where he had been wounded. It was really incredible for him to find himself there. Anyone who would have dared predict such a thing after the armistice of 1918 would have been locked up in an asylum.

"A good guy!" the lieutenant said. "The only way he consoles himself is to realize he'll be too old to fight or, more likely, dead by the time the third one comes around."

"Do you believe that?"

"About the third one? You never know. You find a lot of people today who believe it. We'll know more about it when we've met up with our Red Army friends in Berlin . . ."

The hotel we were heading for was the Hôtel de la Poste. They were all set to welcome us. The first person we met, right in the lobby, was Lieutenant Colonel Marquez.

"What about you, Colonel, do you believe it?"

"Believe what?"

"That there'll be a third world war, of course!"

"Oh!" exclaimed Lieutenant Colonel Marquez, telling us *in his own words*, "don't spoil my dinner!"

And with that, he turned his back on us and departed.

———

. . . At dinner it was easy to imagine I was back in the military court. At one end of the table Lieutenant Colonel Marquez seemed to be presiding, sitting between two officers I had often seen beside him in the hearings. Lieutenant Bradford was there too, still just as young and elegant, quite distinguished-looking. It was like a reenactment at which only the defendant and the witnesses were missing—whether that unfortunate farmer whose wife had been killed, or that little black kid from Harlem whose face, lit up by flashlights in the middle of the night, had looked like that of an idol.

Everything I had seen came back to me. I had been a witness, and I told myself that one day, I in turn might again raise my right hand and say, "I swear!" With one exception, of course, the trial of the Ranger officer who had killed the Resistance fighter—the one I hadn't attended. The killer.

As a matter of fact, why wasn't he sitting there at the table, just as I'd seen him sitting at the mess hall right after his acquittal?

Everyone ate with gusto. They had brought in American foods—pasteurized—and large pitchers of hot chocolate, Nescafé, pastries.

Lieutenant Stone, my neighbor, went on with the story of the American officer who had rediscovered the place where he had been wounded in 1918. It was a real love story. As soon as his wounds had healed, this officer had gone to Paris, and there he had met a young woman with whom he lived for an entire year. It was the greatest memory of his life. When he spoke of it, even now he had tears in his eyes. Just think of it, a Frenchwoman! But, alas, love doesn't last forever!

We listened to him in silence, a little embarrassed. How many at this table had had the same dream? And wasn't war also a great supplier of adventures?

"Oh, God, how romantic!" someone said.

And with that, the racket, the confusion of conversations started up again, and suddenly Lieutenant Stone turned to me.

"You're not saying anything, Louis. Are you all right?"

"Yes, I'm fine."

"You're not sick?"

"Who, me?"

"I really didn't think you looked well this morning. Aren't you eating?"

———

. . . Why bother to describe the rest of the evening? Nothing in the least worth mentioning was said.

When we got up from the table, Lieutenant Stone dragged me toward one of the officers.

"Here's our interpreter," he said. "I don't think he's in good shape. And I'm the one who brought him into the army. I'd like you to tell me whether he can continue traveling with us, whether I can take that responsibility."

From the conversation we had with that superior officer, it turned out they couldn't take that responsibility.